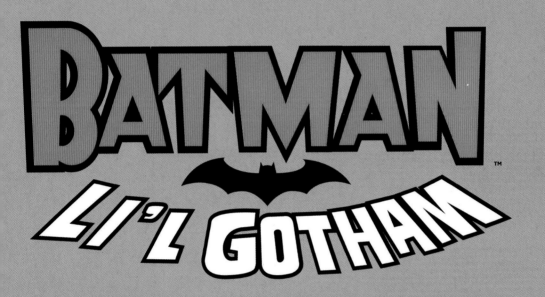

BATMAN™

LI'L GOTHAM

STONE ARCH BOOKS
a capstone imprint

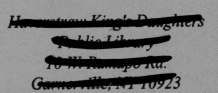

▼▼ STONE ARCH BOOKS™

Published in 2014 by Stone Arch Books
A Capstone Imprint
1710 Roe Crest Drive
North Mankato, MN 56003
www.capstonepub.com

Originally published by DC Comics in the U.S. in single
magazine form as Batman: Li'l Gotham.
Copyright © 2014 DC Comics. All Rights Reserved.

DC Comics
1700 Broadway, New York, NY 10019
A Warner Bros. Entertainment Company

Printed in China.
032014   008085LEOF14

Cataloging-in-Publication Data is available at the Library
of Congress website:
ISBN: 978-1-4342-9217-9 (library binding)

Summary: It's Christmas, meaning Gotham's annual
tree-lighting ceremony is near. But when the children's
choir goes missing from the celebration, it's up to Batman
and Nightwing to track down the culprit and free the
children. Then, on New Year's Eve, Catwoman resolves to
turn over a new leaf and leave her life of crime behind...
until her pals Poison Ivy and Harley Quinn show up for
a girl's night out!

STONE ARCH BOOKS
Ashley C. Andersen Zantop Publisher
Michael Dahl Editorial Director
Sean Tulien Editor
Heather Kindseth Creative Director
Bob Lentz Art Director
Hilary Wacholz Designer
Kathy McColley Production Specialist

DC Comics
Sarah Gaydos Original U.S. Editor

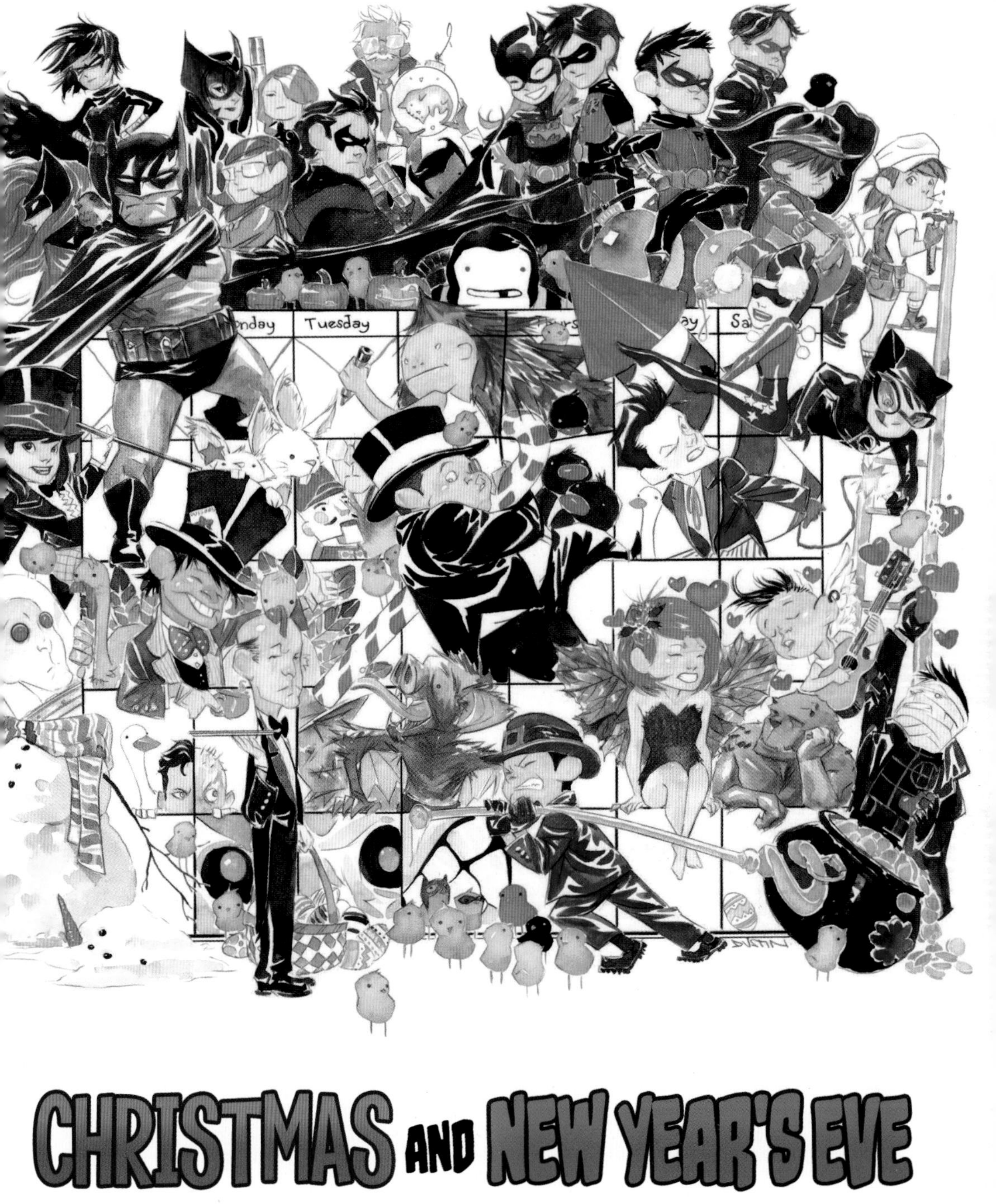
Tuesday
DUSTIN

CHRISTMAS AND NEW YEAR'S EVE

Dustin Nguyen & Derek Fridolfs....................... writers
Dustin Nguyen.. artist
Saida Temofonte.. letterer

BATMAN created by
Bob Kane

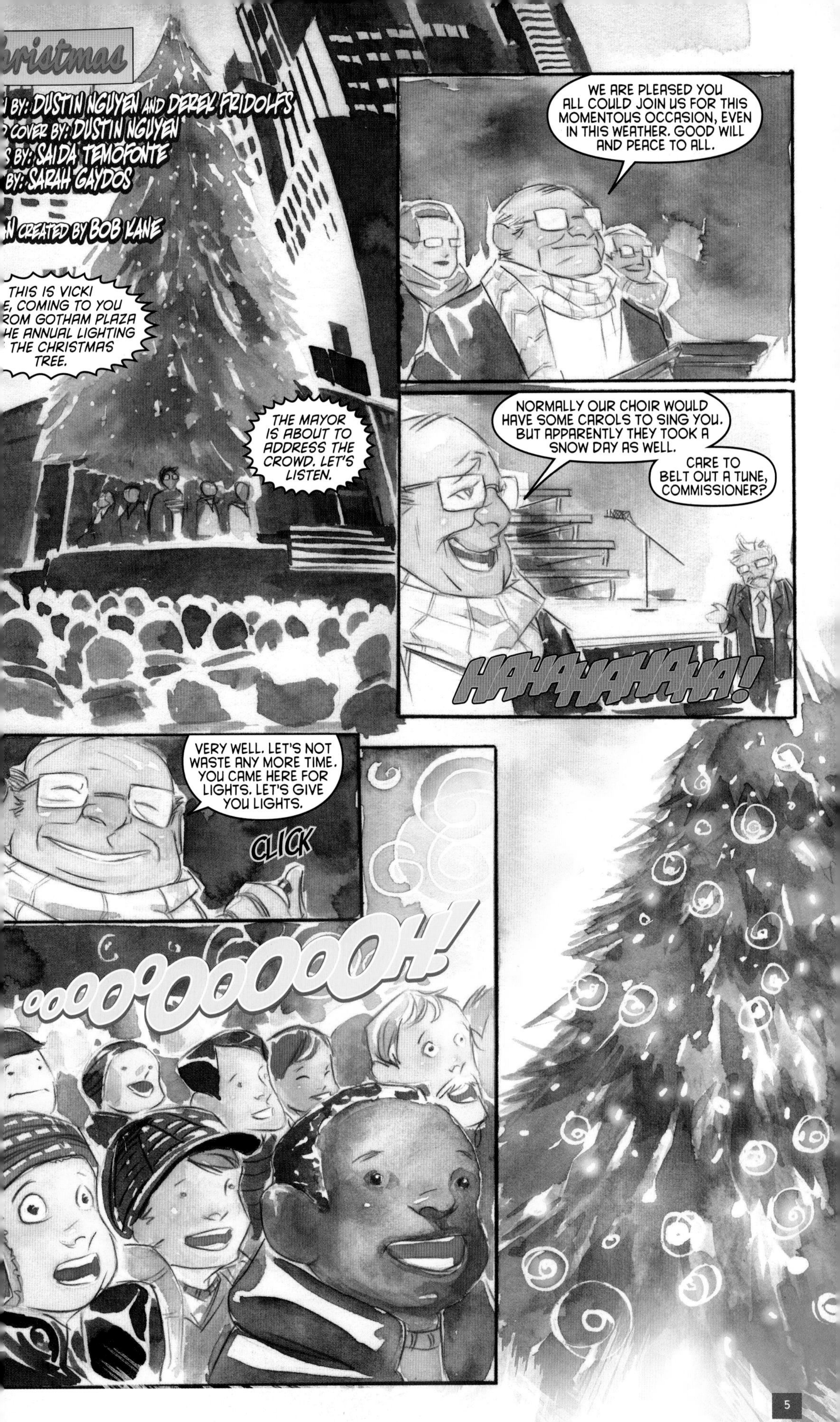

...hristmas
...N BY: DUSTIN NGUYEN AND DEREK FRIDOLFS
...D COVER BY: DUSTIN NGUYEN
...S BY: SAIDA TEMOFONTE
... BY: SARAH GAYDOS
...N CREATED BY BOB KANE
THIS IS VICKI ...E, COMING TO YOU ...ROM GOTHAM PLAZA ...HE ANNUAL LIGHTING ... THE CHRISTMAS TREE.
THE MAYOR IS ABOUT TO ADDRESS THE CROWD. LET'S LISTEN.
WE ARE PLEASED YOU ALL COULD JOIN US FOR THIS MOMENTOUS OCCASION, EVEN IN THIS WEATHER. GOOD WILL AND PEACE TO ALL.
NORMALLY OUR CHOIR WOULD HAVE SOME CAROLS TO SING YOU. BUT APPARENTLY THEY TOOK A SNOW DAY AS WELL.
CARE TO BELT OUT A TUNE, COMMISSIONER?
HAHAHAHAHAHA!
VERY WELL. LET'S NOT WASTE ANY MORE TIME. YOU CAME HERE FOR LIGHTS. LET'S GIVE YOU LIGHTS.
CLICK
OOOOOOOOOOH!

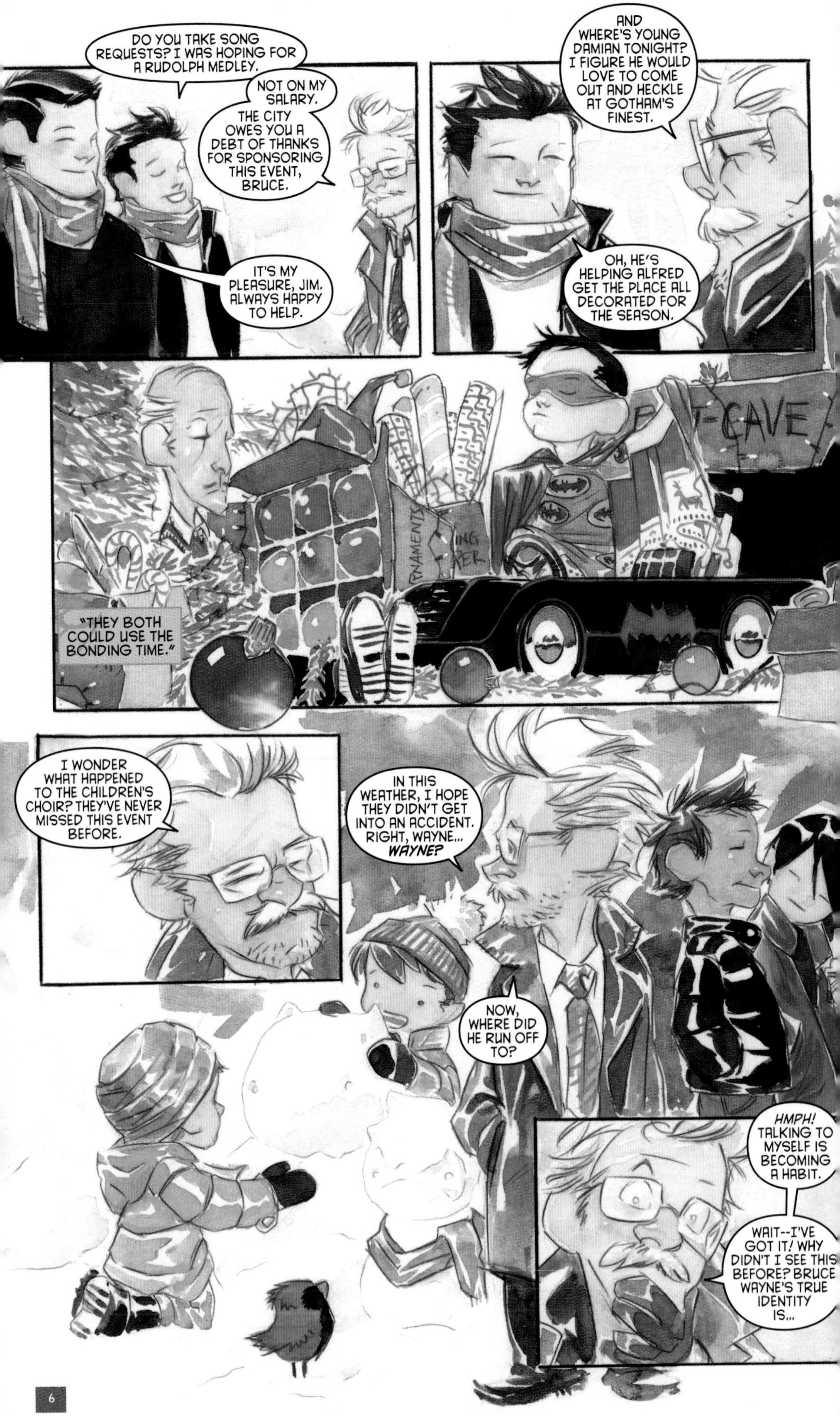
DO YOU TAKE SONG REQUESTS? I WAS HOPING FOR A RUDOLPH MEDLEY.
NOT ON MY SALARY.
THE CITY OWES YOU A DEBT OF THANKS FOR SPONSORING THIS EVENT, BRUCE.
IT'S MY PLEASURE, JIM. ALWAYS HAPPY TO HELP.
AND WHERE'S YOUNG DAMIAN TONIGHT? I FIGURE HE WOULD LOVE TO COME OUT AND HECKLE AT GOTHAM'S FINEST.
OH, HE'S HELPING ALFRED GET THE PLACE ALL DECORATED FOR THE SEASON.
-CAVE
RNAMENTS
ING
PER
"THEY BOTH COULD USE THE BONDING TIME."
I WONDER WHAT HAPPENED TO THE CHILDREN'S CHOIR? THEY'VE NEVER MISSED THIS EVENT BEFORE.
IN THIS WEATHER, I HOPE THEY DIDN'T GET INTO AN ACCIDENT. RIGHT, WAYNE... *WAYNE?*
NOW, WHERE DID HE RUN OFF TO?
HMPH! TALKING TO MYSELF IS BECOMING A HABIT.
WAIT--I'VE GOT IT! WHY DIDN'T I SEE THIS BEFORE? BRUCE WAYNE'S TRUE IDENTITY IS...

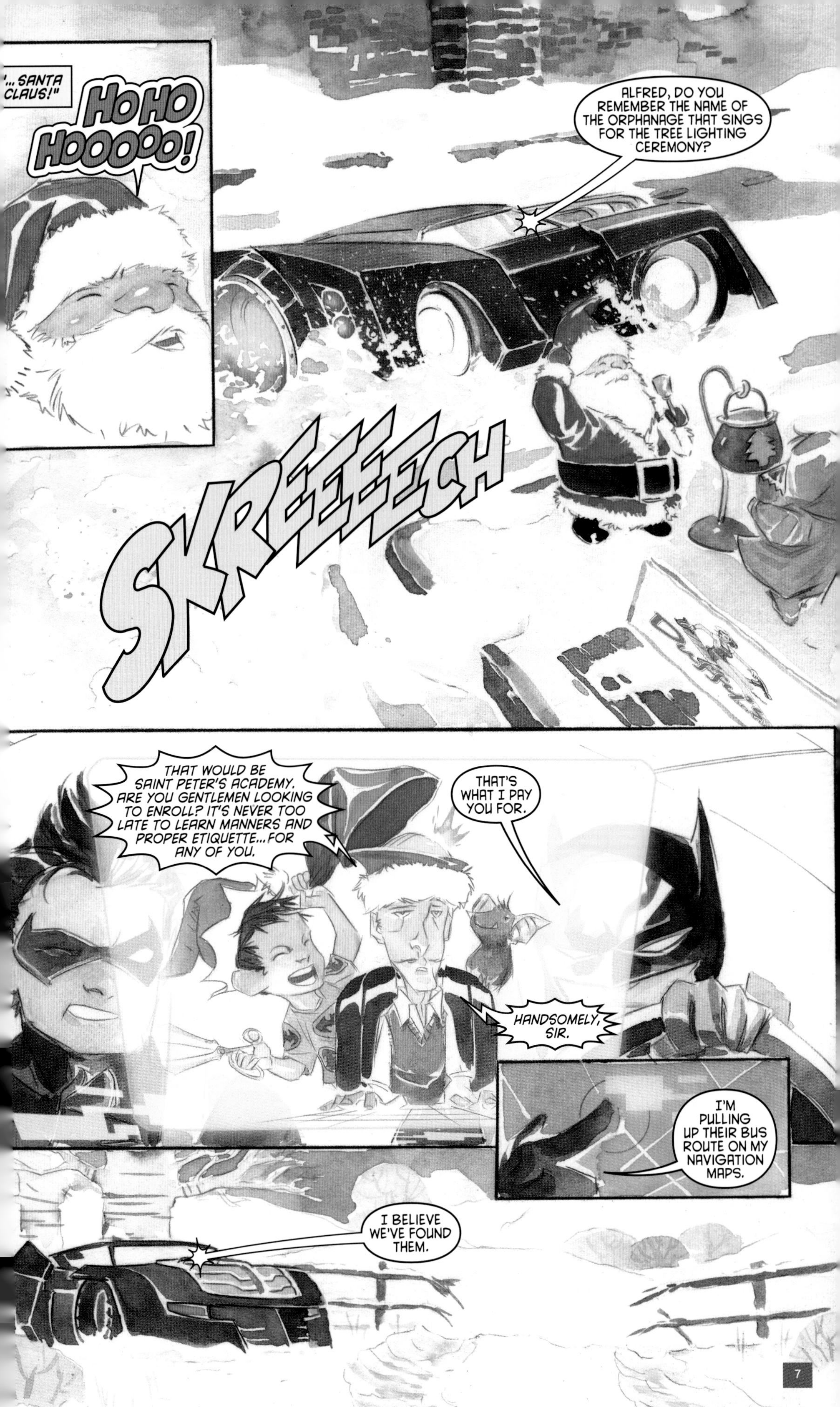
"...SANTA CLAUS!"
HO HO HOOOOO!
ALFRED, DO YOU REMEMBER THE NAME OF THE ORPHANAGE THAT SINGS FOR THE TREE LIGHTING CEREMONY?
SKREEEECH
THAT WOULD BE SAINT PETER'S ACADEMY. ARE YOU GENTLEMEN LOOKING TO ENROLL? IT'S NEVER TOO LATE TO LEARN MANNERS AND PROPER ETIQUETTE...FOR ANY OF YOU.
THAT'S WHAT I PAY YOU FOR.
HANDSOMELY, SIR.
I'M PULLING UP THEIR BUS ROUTE ON MY NAVIGATION MAPS.
I BELIEVE WE'VE FOUND THEM.

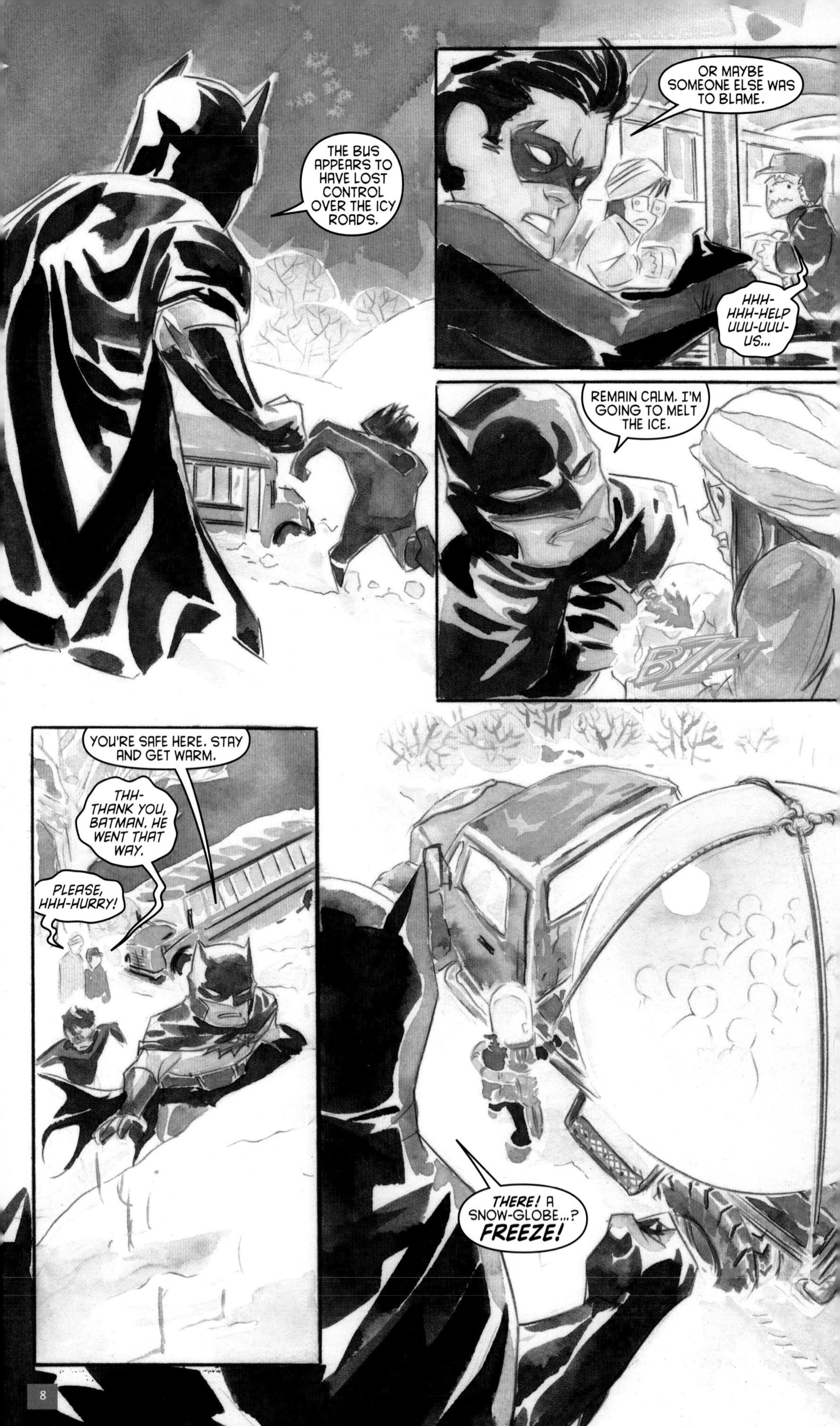
THE BUS APPEARS TO HAVE LOST CONTROL OVER THE ICY ROADS.
OR MAYBE SOMEONE ELSE WAS TO BLAME.
HHH-HHH-HELP UUU-UUU-US...
REMAIN CALM. I'M GOING TO MELT THE ICE.
BZZT
YOU'RE SAFE HERE. STAY AND GET WARM.
THH-THANK YOU, BATMAN. HE WENT THAT WAY.
PLEASE, HHH-HURRY!
THERE! A SNOW-GLOBE...? FREEZE!

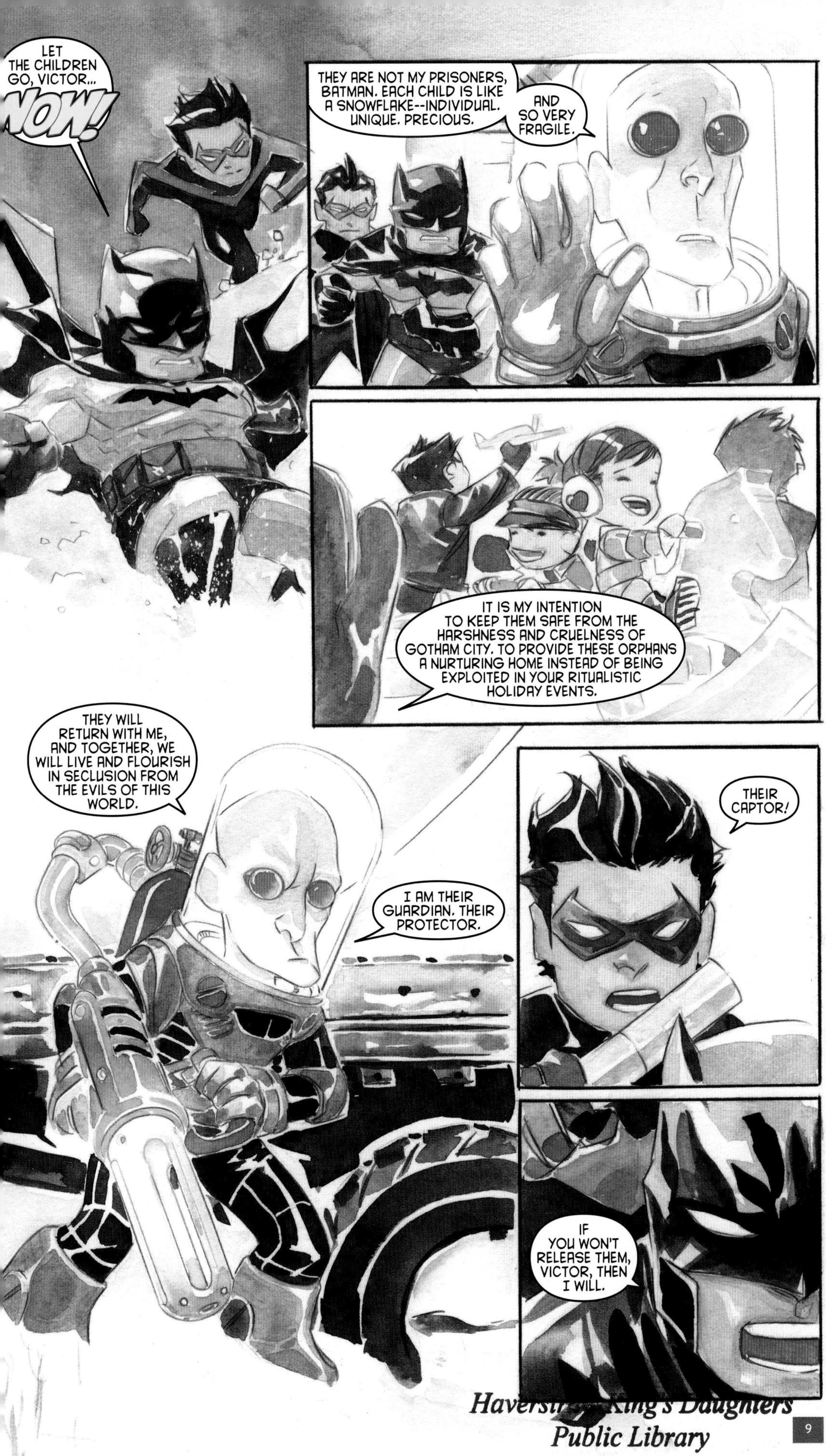

LET THE CHILDREN GO, VICTOR... NOW!
THEY ARE NOT MY PRISONERS, BATMAN. EACH CHILD IS LIKE A SNOWFLAKE--INDIVIDUAL. UNIQUE. PRECIOUS.
AND SO VERY FRAGILE.
IT IS MY INTENTION TO KEEP THEM SAFE FROM THE HARSHNESS AND CRUELNESS OF GOTHAM CITY. TO PROVIDE THESE ORPHANS A NURTURING HOME INSTEAD OF BEING EXPLOITED IN YOUR RITUALISTIC HOLIDAY EVENTS.
THEY WILL RETURN WITH ME, AND TOGETHER, WE WILL LIVE AND FLOURISH IN SECLUSION FROM THE EVILS OF THIS WORLD.
I AM THEIR GUARDIAN. THEIR PROTECTOR.
THEIR CAPTOR!
IF YOU WON'T RELEASE THEM, VICTOR, THEN I WILL.

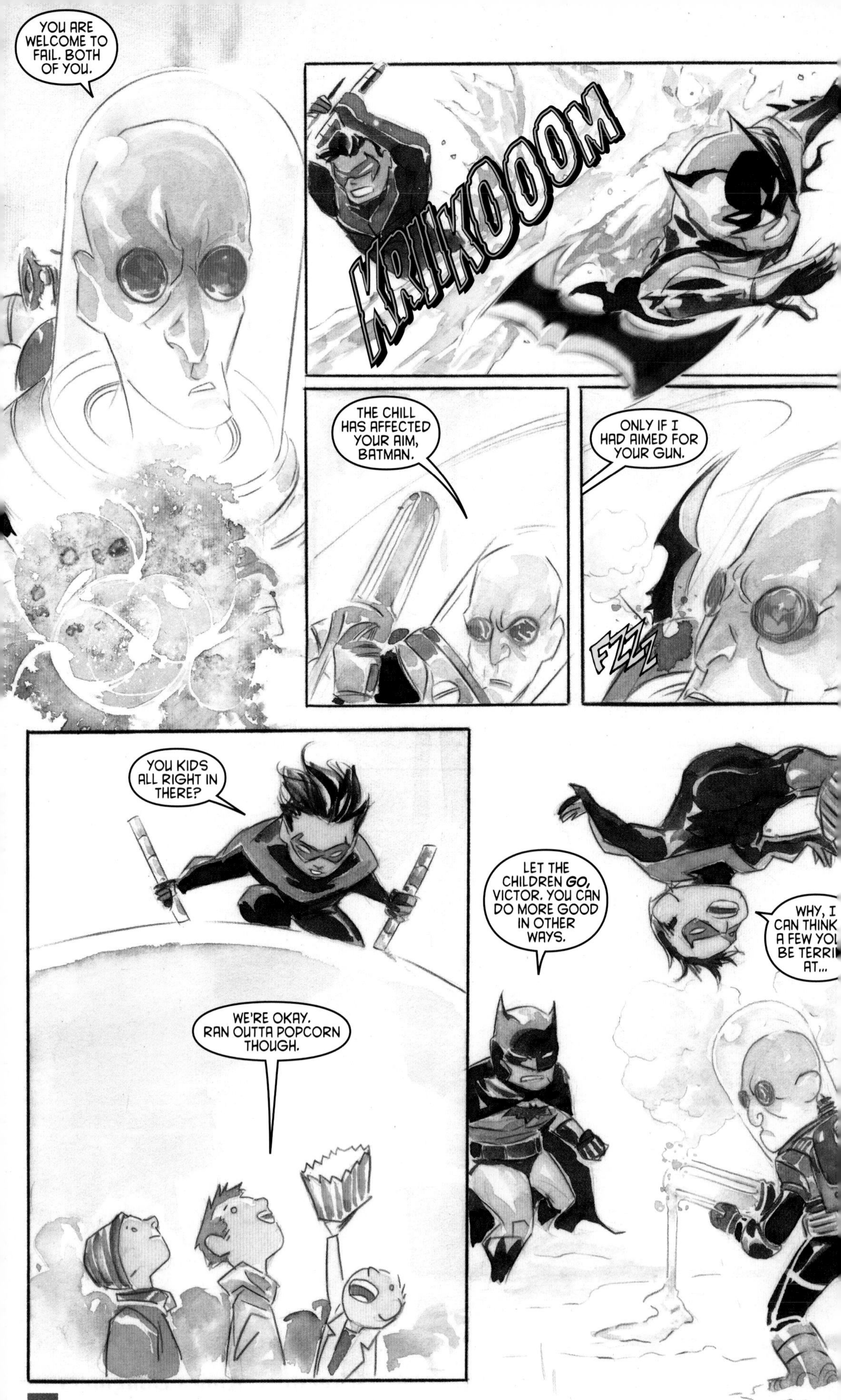
YOU ARE WELCOME TO FAIL. BOTH OF YOU.
KRIIKOOOM
THE CHILL HAS AFFECTED YOUR AIM, BATMAN.
ONLY IF I HAD AIMED FOR YOUR GUN.
FZZZ
YOU KIDS ALL RIGHT IN THERE?
WE'RE OKAY. RAN OUTTA POPCORN THOUGH.
LET THE CHILDREN GO, VICTOR. YOU CAN DO MORE GOOD IN OTHER WAYS.

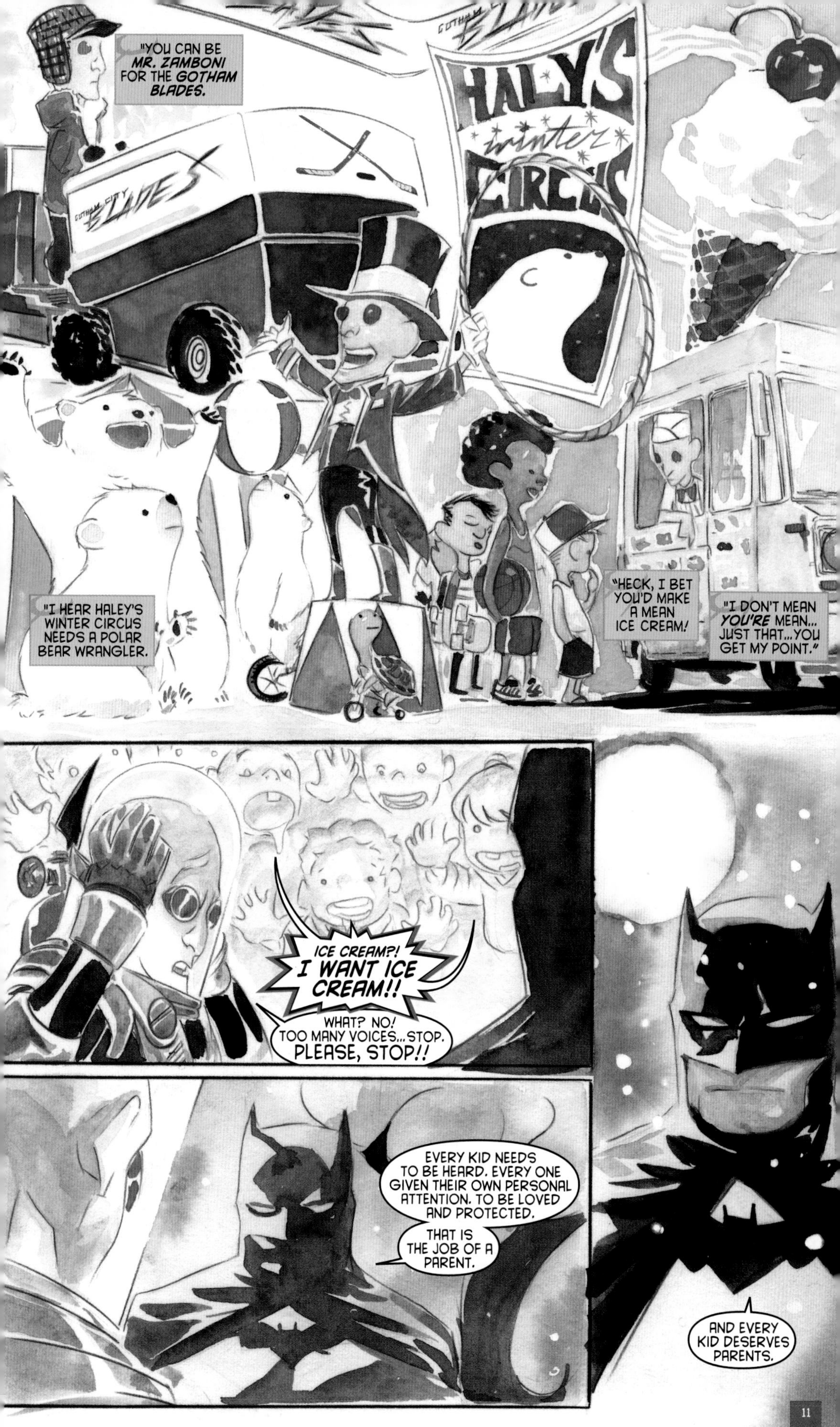
"YOU CAN BE MR. ZAMBONI FOR THE GOTHAM BLADES.
HALY'S winter CIRCUS
GOTHAM CITY BLADES
"I HEAR HALEY'S WINTER CIRCUS NEEDS A POLAR BEAR WRANGLER.
"HECK, I BET YOU'D MAKE A MEAN ICE CREAM!
"I DON'T MEAN YOU'RE MEAN... JUST THAT... YOU GET MY POINT."
ICE CREAM?! I WANT ICE CREAM!!
WHAT? NO! TOO MANY VOICES... STOP. PLEASE, STOP!!
EVERY KID NEEDS TO BE HEARD. EVERY ONE GIVEN THEIR OWN PERSONAL ATTENTION. TO BE LOVED AND PROTECTED.
THAT IS THE JOB OF A PARENT.
AND EVERY KID DESERVES PARENTS.

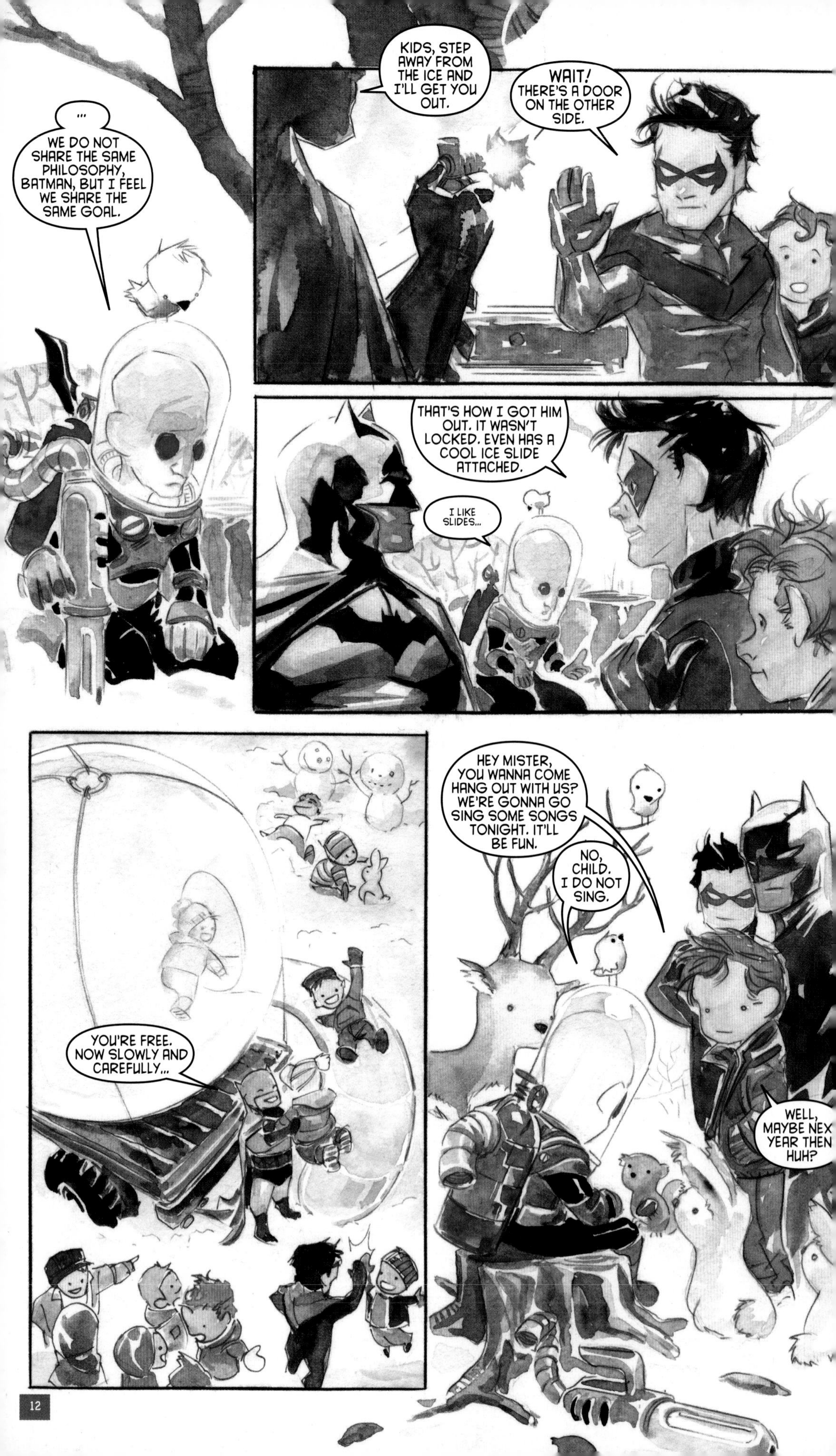

...
WE DO NOT SHARE THE SAME PHILOSOPHY, BATMAN, BUT I FEEL WE SHARE THE SAME GOAL.
KIDS, STEP AWAY FROM THE ICE AND I'LL GET YOU OUT.
WAIT! THERE'S A DOOR ON THE OTHER SIDE.
THAT'S HOW I GOT HIM OUT. IT WASN'T LOCKED. EVEN HAS A COOL ICE SLIDE ATTACHED.
I LIKE SLIDES...
YOU'RE FREE. NOW SLOWLY AND CAREFULLY...
HEY MISTER, YOU WANNA COME HANG OUT WITH US? WE'RE GONNA GO SING SOME SONGS TONIGHT. IT'LL BE FUN.
NO, CHILD. I DO NOT SING.
WELL, MAYBE NEX YEAR THEN HUH?

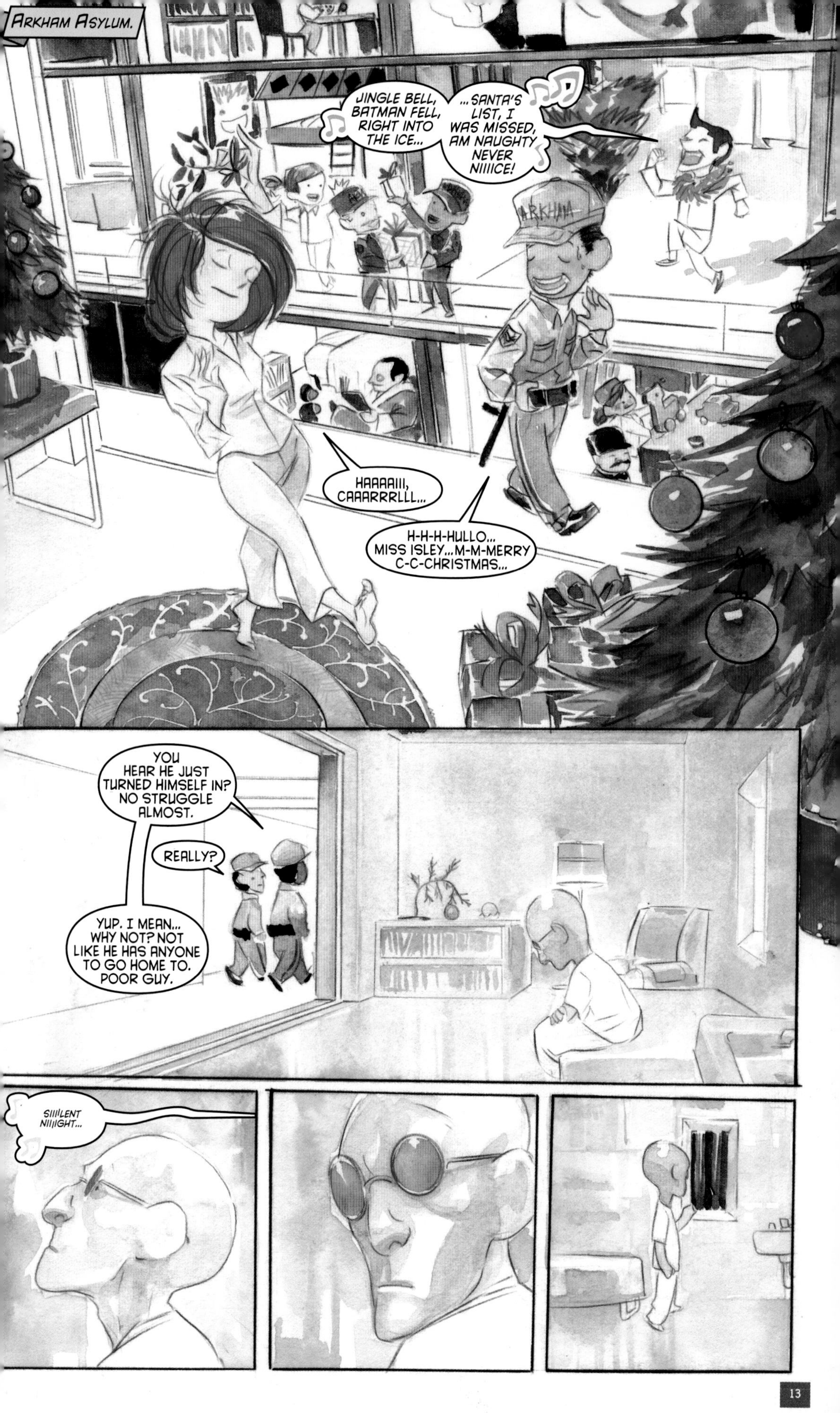

ARKHAM ASYLUM.
JINGLE BELL, BATMAN FELL, RIGHT INTO THE ICE...
...SANTA'S LIST, I WAS MISSED, AM NAUGHTY NEVER NIIIICE!
HAAAAIII, CAAARRRLLL...
H-H-H-HULLO... MISS ISLEY...M-M-MERRY C-C-CHRISTMAS...
YOU HEAR HE JUST TURNED HIMSELF IN? NO STRUGGLE ALMOST.
REALLY?
YUP. I MEAN... WHY NOT? NOT LIKE HE HAS ANYONE TO GO HOME TO. POOR GUY.
SIIIILENT NIIIIGHT...

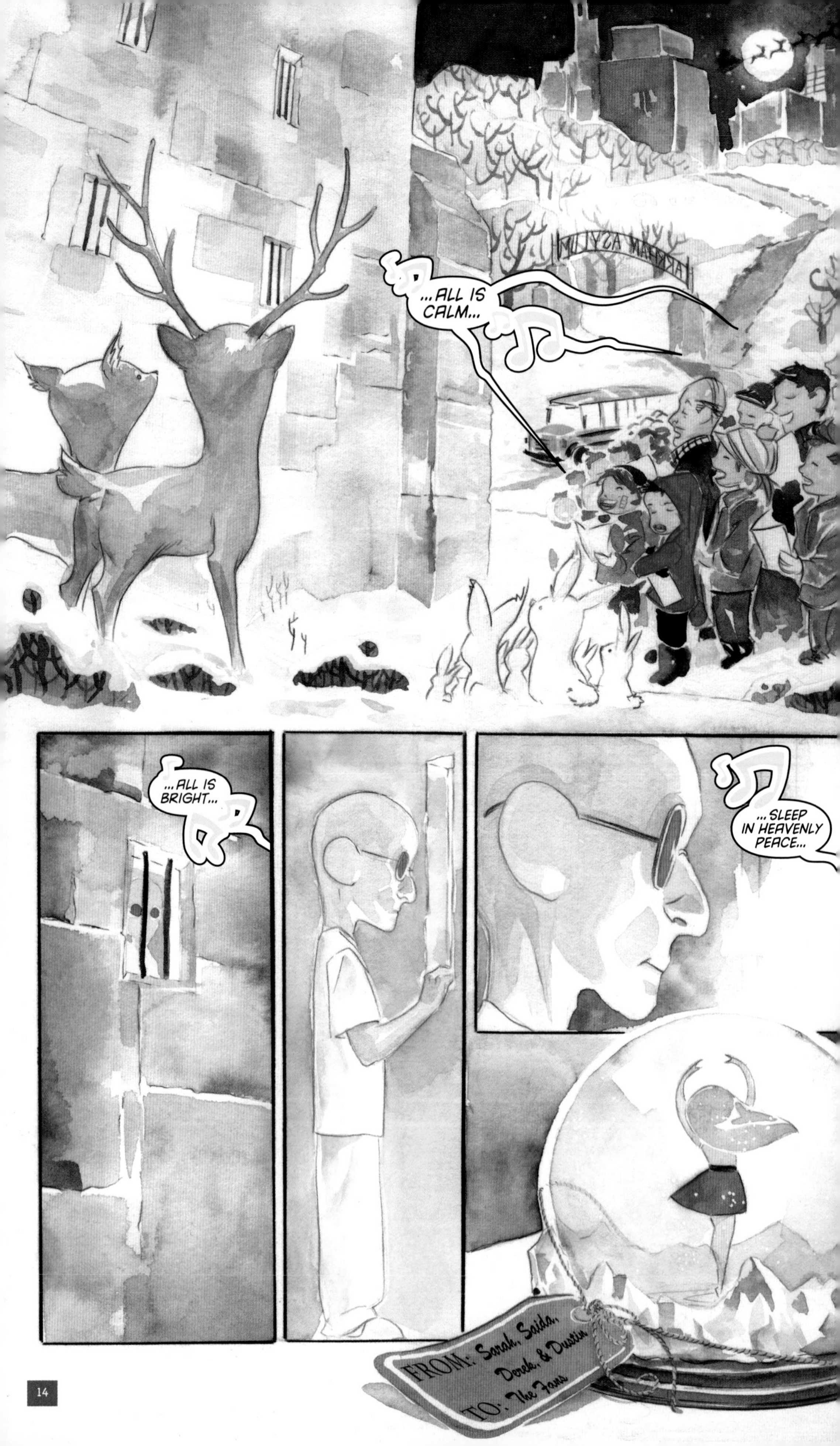
ARKHAM ASYLUM
...ALL IS CALM...
...ALL IS BRIGHT...
...SLEEP IN HEAVENLY PEACE...
FROM: Sarah, Saida, Derek, & Dustin
TO: The Fans

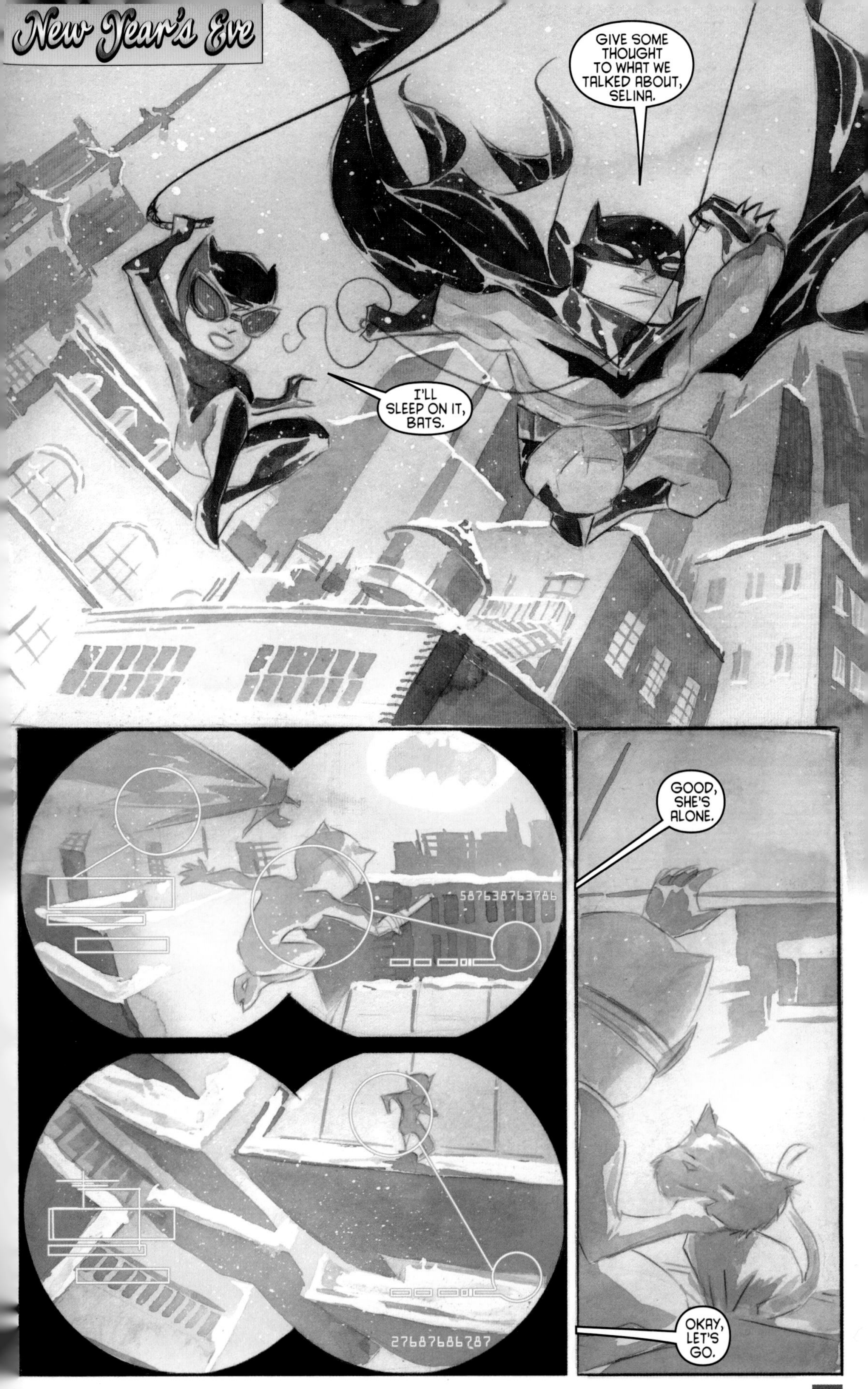

New Year's Eve
GIVE SOME THOUGHT TO WHAT WE TALKED ABOUT, SELINA.
I'LL SLEEP ON IT, BATS.
58763876378б
27687686787
GOOD, SHE'S ALONE.
OKAY, LET'S GO.

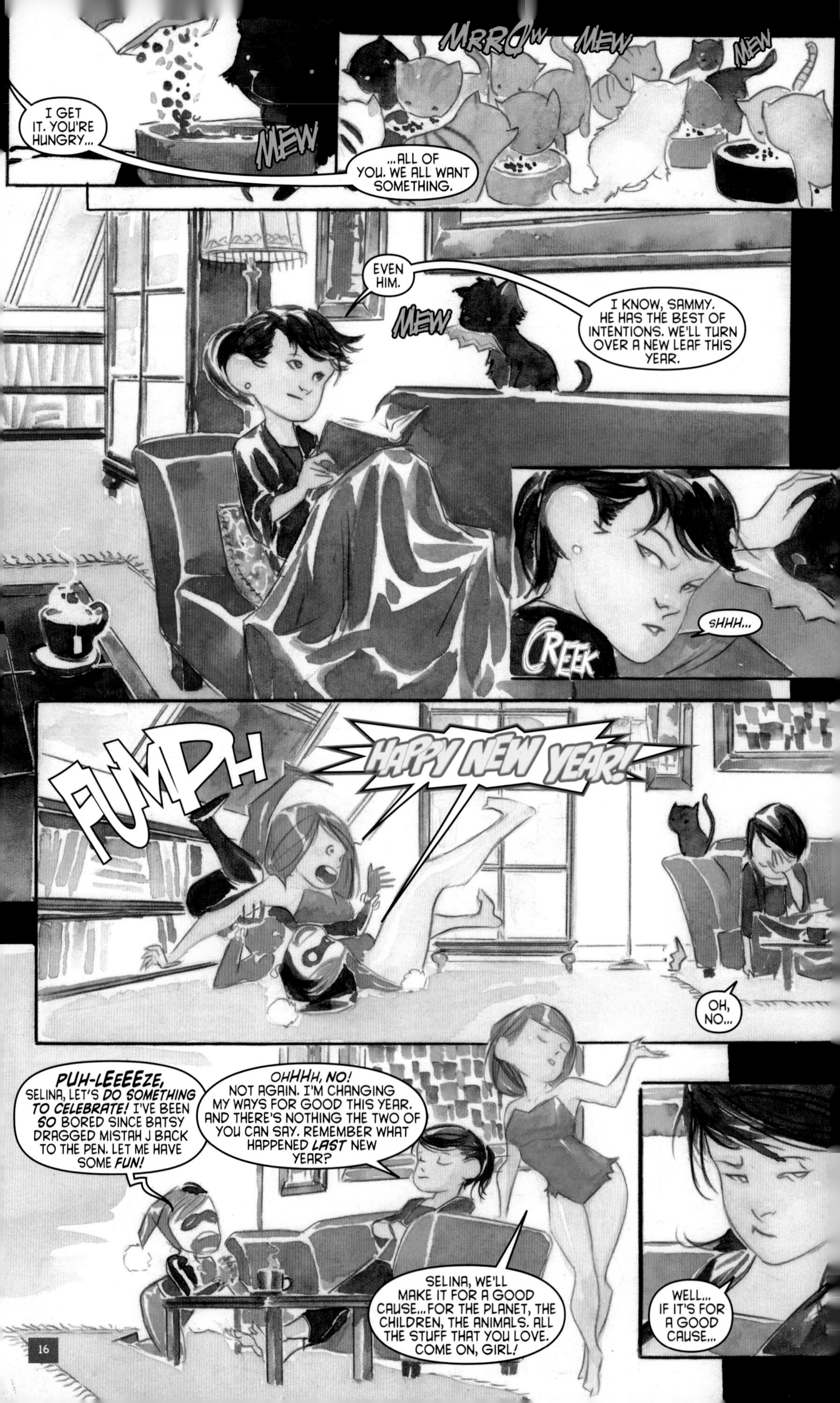

I GET IT. YOU'RE HUNGRY...
MEW
MRROW
MEW
MEW
...ALL OF YOU. WE ALL WANT SOMETHING.
EVEN HIM.
MEW
I KNOW, SAMMY. HE HAS THE BEST OF INTENTIONS. WE'LL TURN OVER A NEW LEAF THIS YEAR.
CREEK
SHHH...
FUMPH
HAPPY NEW YEAR!
OH, NO...
PUH-LEEEEZE, SELINA, LET'S DO SOMETHING TO CELEBRATE! I'VE BEEN SO BORED SINCE BATSY DRAGGED MISTAH J BACK TO THE PEN. LET ME HAVE SOME FUN!
OHHHH, NO! NOT AGAIN. I'M CHANGING MY WAYS FOR GOOD THIS YEAR. AND THERE'S NOTHING THE TWO OF YOU CAN SAY. REMEMBER WHAT HAPPENED LAST NEW YEAR?
SELINA, WE'LL MAKE IT FOR A GOOD CAUSE...FOR THE PLANET, THE CHILDREN, THE ANIMALS. ALL THE STUFF THAT YOU LOVE. COME ON, GIRL!
WELL... IF IT'S FOR A GOOD CAUSE...

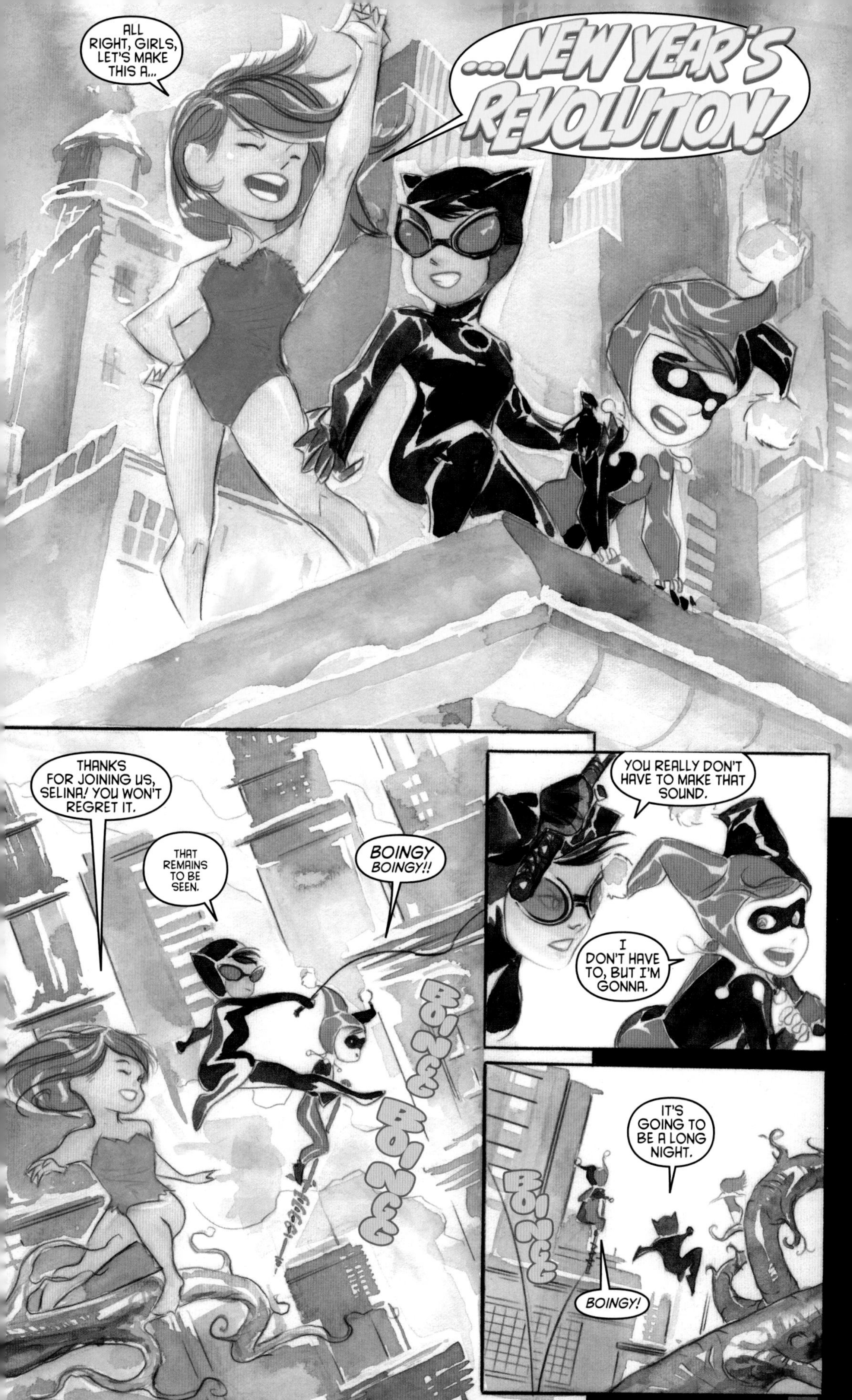

ALL RIGHT, GIRLS, LET'S MAKE THIS A...
...NEW YEAR'S REVOLUTION!
THANKS FOR JOINING US, SELINA! YOU WON'T REGRET IT.
THAT REMAINS TO BE SEEN.
BOINGY BOINGY!!
YOU REALLY DON'T HAVE TO MAKE THAT SOUND.
I DON'T HAVE TO, BUT I'M GONNA.
IT'S GOING TO BE A LONG NIGHT.
BOINGY!

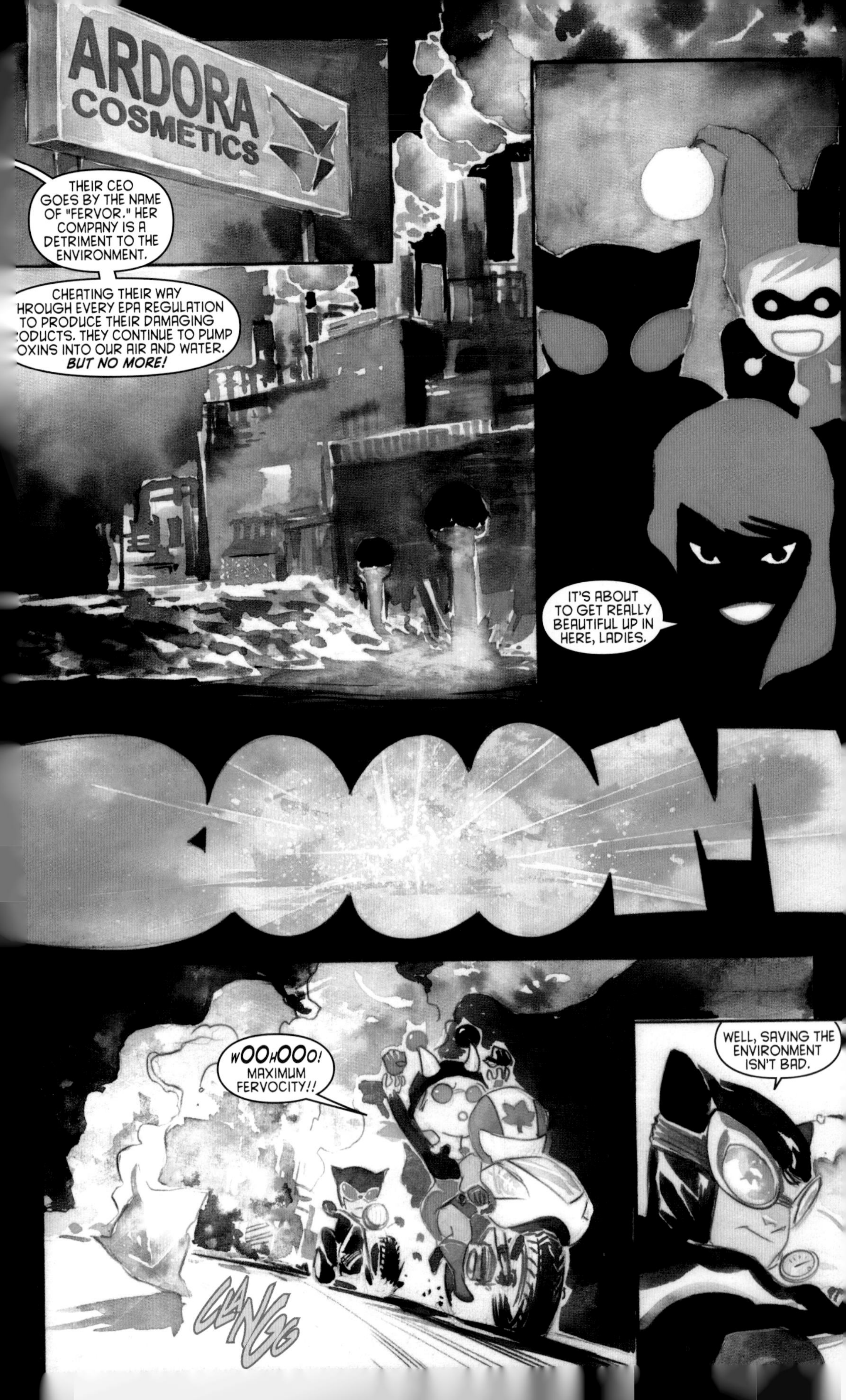
ARDORA COSMETICS
THEIR CEO GOES BY THE NAME OF "FERVOR." HER COMPANY IS A DETRIMENT TO THE ENVIRONMENT.
CHEATING THEIR WAY HROUGH EVERY EPA REGULATION TO PRODUCE THEIR DAMAGING RODUCTS. THEY CONTINUE TO PUMP OXINS INTO OUR AIR AND WATER. *BUT NO MORE!*
IT'S ABOUT TO GET REALLY BEAUTIFUL UP IN HERE, LADIES.
WOOHOOO! MAXIMUM FERVOCITY!!
WELL, SAVING THE ENVIRONMENT ISN'T BAD.

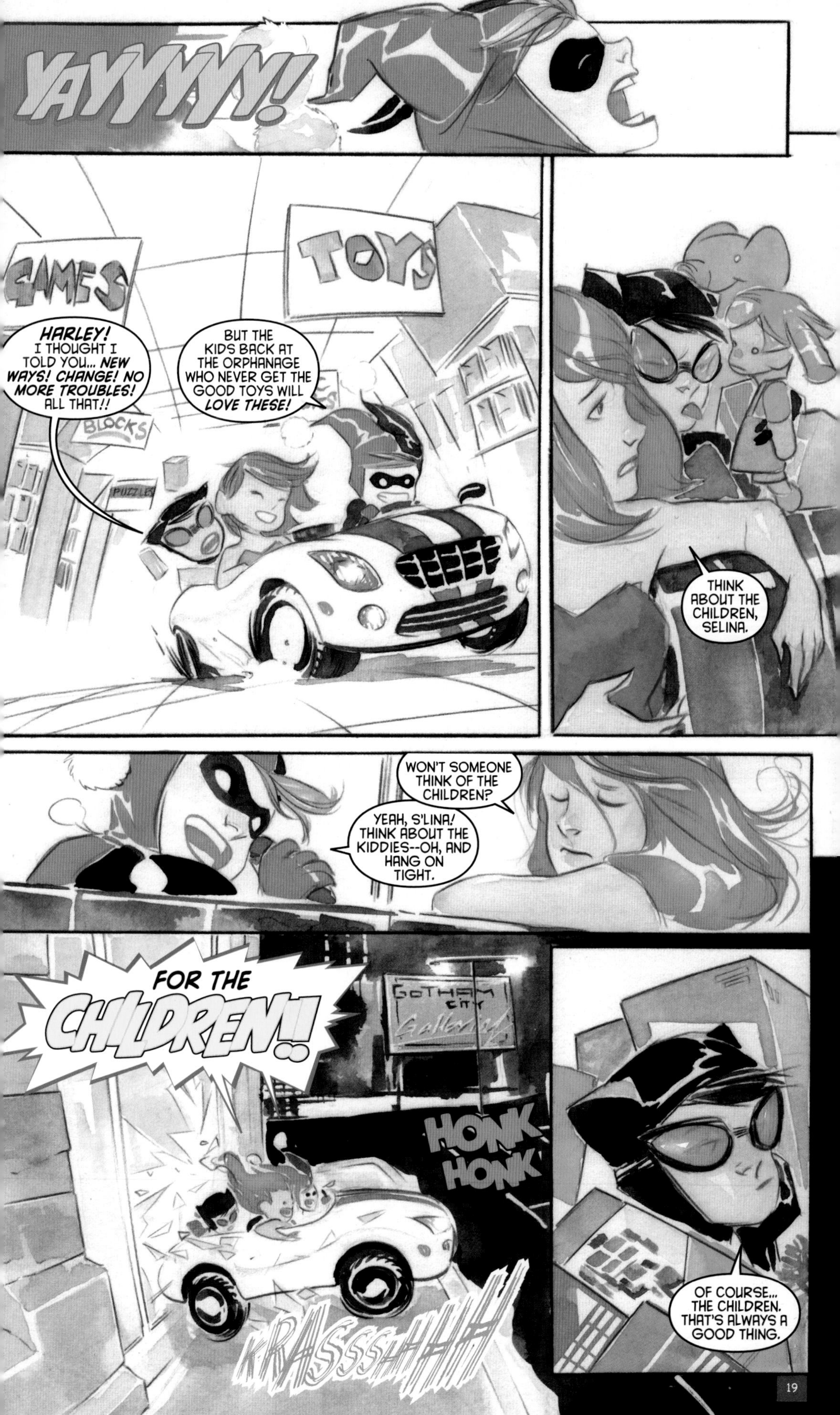
YAYYYYY!
GAMES
TOYS
BLOCKS
PUZZLES
HARLEY! I THOUGHT I TOLD YOU... NEW WAYS! CHANGE! NO MORE TROUBLES! ALL THAT!!
BUT THE KIDS BACK AT THE ORPHANAGE WHO NEVER GET THE GOOD TOYS WILL LOVE THESE!
THINK ABOUT THE CHILDREN, SELINA.
WON'T SOMEONE THINK OF THE CHILDREN?
YEAH, S'LINA! THINK ABOUT THE KIDDIES--OH, AND HANG ON TIGHT.
FOR THE CHILDREN!!
GOTHAM CITY Gallery
HONK HONK
KRASSSHHHH
OF COURSE... THE CHILDREN. THAT'S ALWAYS A GOOD THING.

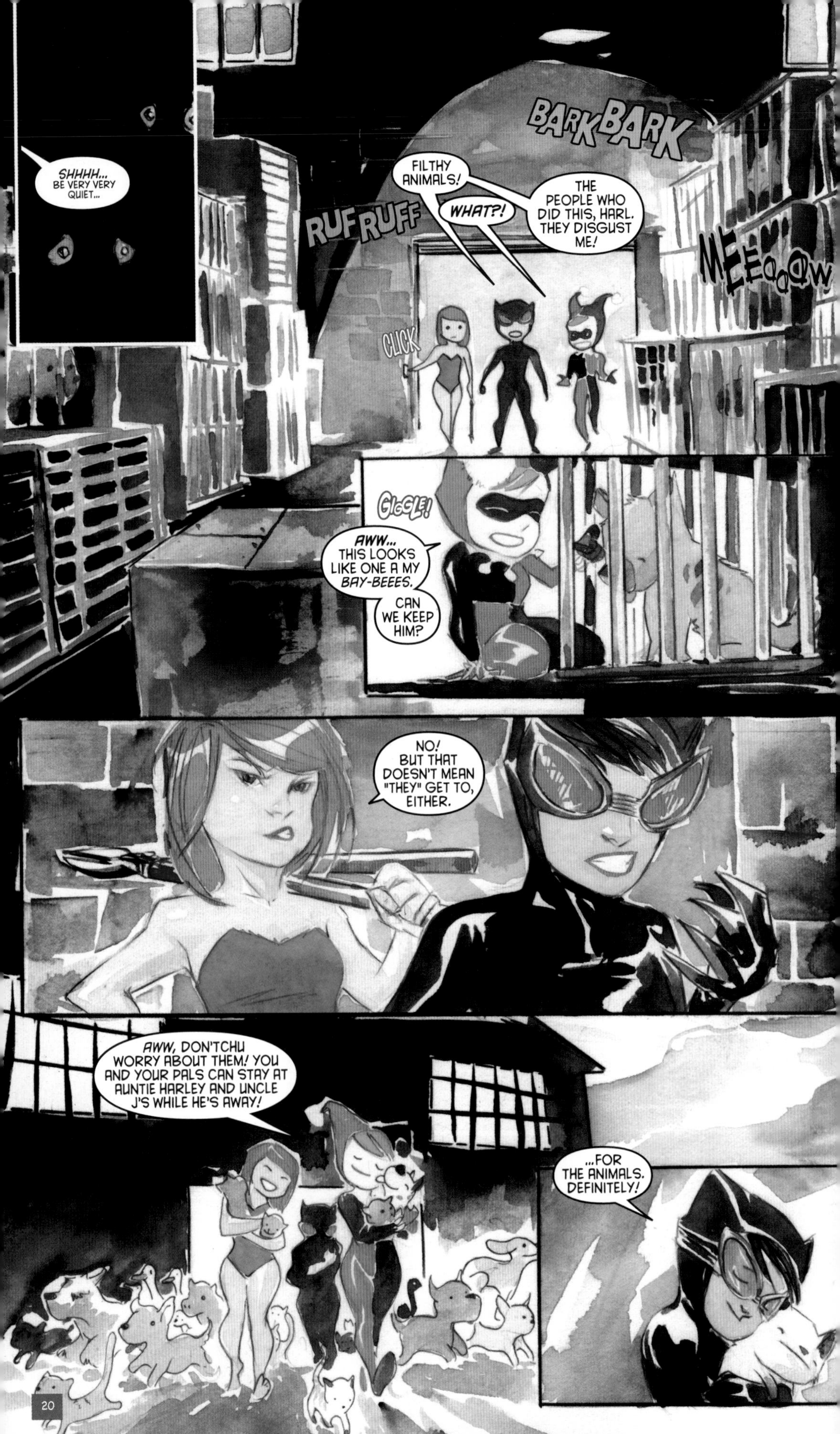

SHHHH... BE VERY VERY QUIET...
BARK BARK
FILTHY ANIMALS!
RUF RUFF
WHAT?!
THE PEOPLE WHO DID THIS, HARL. THEY DISGUST ME!
MEEOOW
CLICK
GIGGLE!
AWW... THIS LOOKS LIKE ONE A MY BAY-BEEES.
CAN WE KEEP HIM?
NO! BUT THAT DOESN'T MEAN "THEY" GET TO, EITHER.
AWW, DON'TCHU WORRY ABOUT THEM! YOU AND YOUR PALS CAN STAY AT AUNTIE HARLEY AND UNCLE J'S WHILE HE'S AWAY!
...FOR THE ANIMALS. DEFINITELY!

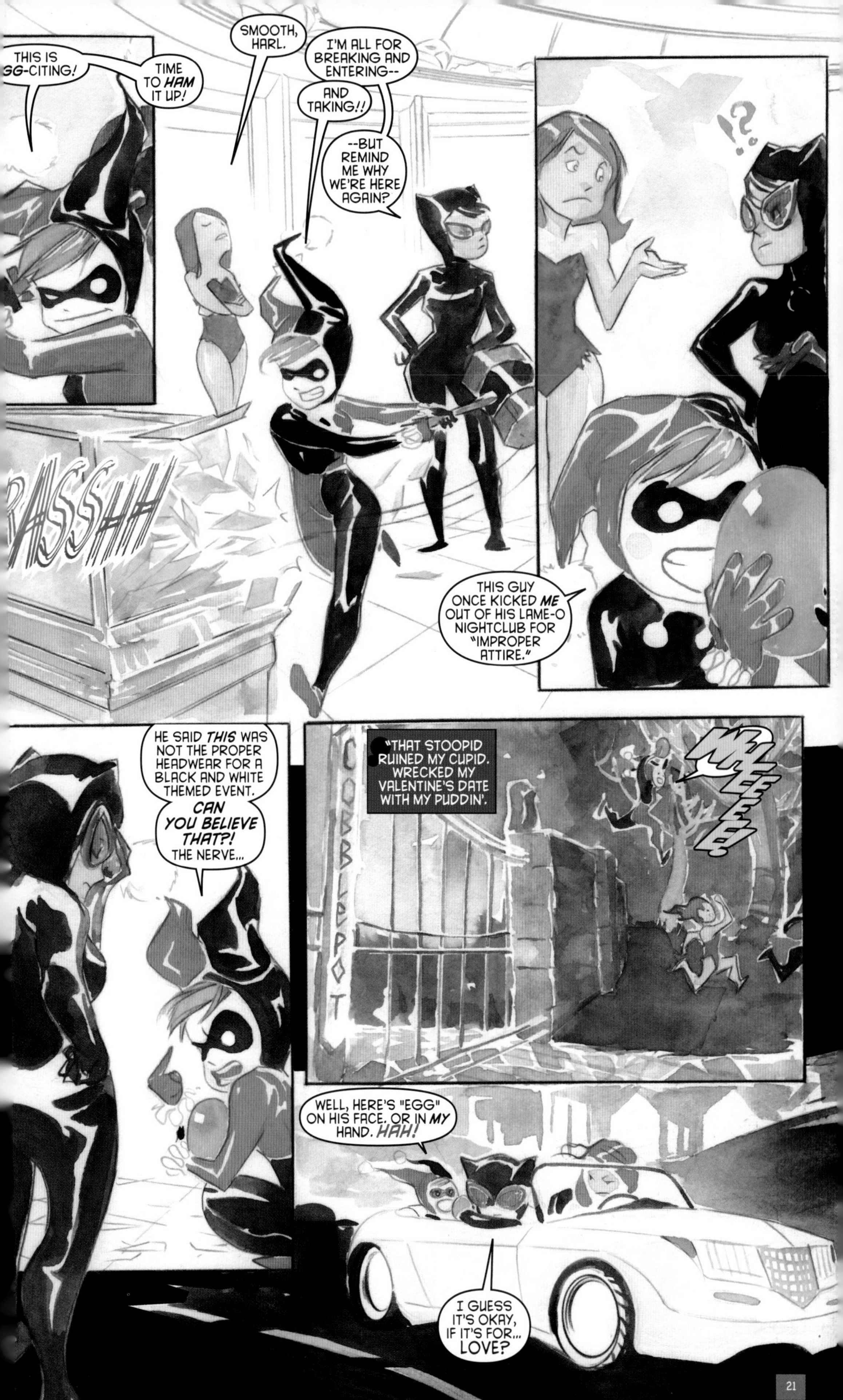

THIS IS EGG-CITING!
TIME TO HAM IT UP!
SMOOTH, HARL.
I'M ALL FOR BREAKING AND ENTERING--
AND TAKING!!
--BUT REMIND ME WHY WE'RE HERE AGAIN?
RASSHH
?!
THIS GUY ONCE KICKED ME OUT OF HIS LAME-O NIGHTCLUB FOR "IMPROPER ATTIRE."
HE SAID THIS WAS NOT THE PROPER HEADWEAR FOR A BLACK AND WHITE THEMED EVENT.
CAN YOU BELIEVE THAT?! THE NERVE...
"THAT STOOPID RUINED MY CUPID. WRECKED MY VALENTINE'S DATE WITH MY PUDDIN'.
COBBLEPOT
WHEEEEE!
WELL, HERE'S "EGG" ON HIS FACE. OR IN MY HAND. HAH!
I GUESS IT'S OKAY, IF IT'S FOR... LOVE?

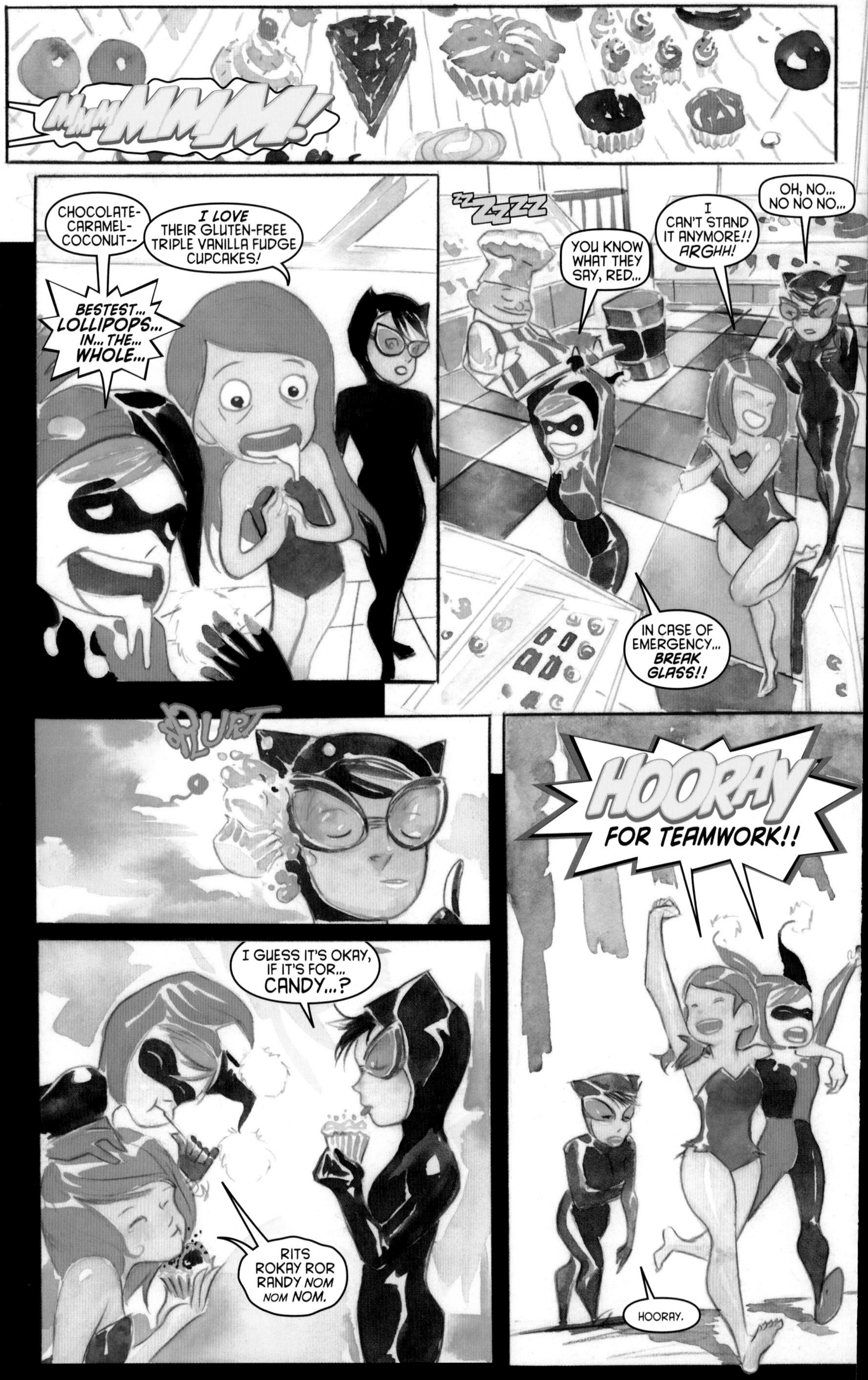
MMMMMM!
CHOCOLATE-CARAMEL-COCONUT--
I LOVE THEIR GLUTEN-FREE TRIPLE VANILLA FUDGE CUPCAKES!
BESTEST... LOLLIPOPS... IN... THE... WHOLE...
ZZZZZ
YOU KNOW WHAT THEY SAY, RED...
I CAN'T STAND IT ANYMORE!! ARGHH!
OH, NO... NO NO NO...
IN CASE OF EMERGENCY... BREAK GLASS!!
SPLURT
HOORAY FOR TEAMWORK!!
I GUESS IT'S OKAY, IF IT'S FOR... CANDY...?
RITS ROKAY ROR RANDY NOM NOM NOM.
HOORAY.

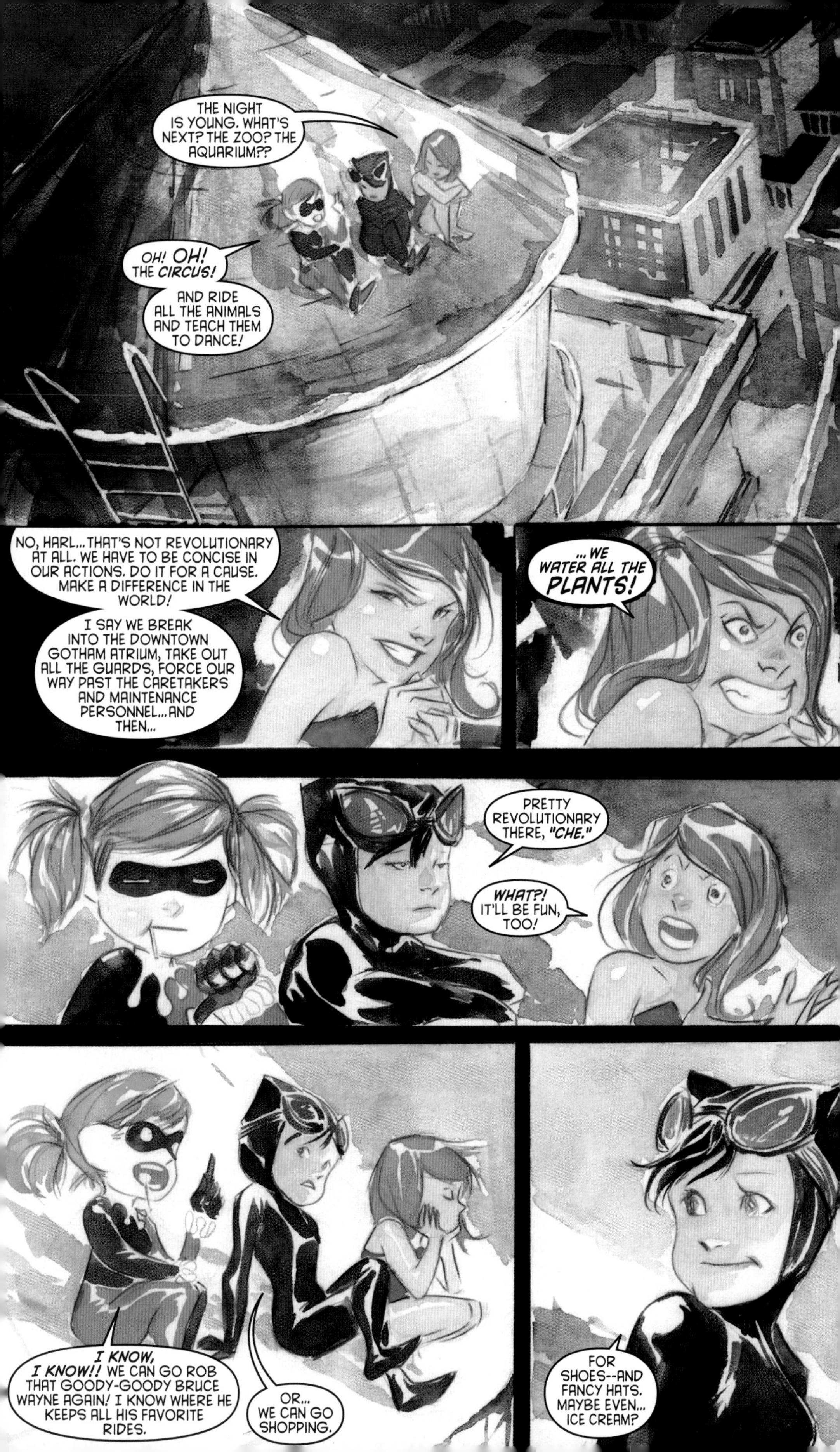
THE NIGHT IS YOUNG. WHAT'S NEXT? THE ZOO? THE AQUARIUM??
OH! OH! THE CIRCUS!
AND RIDE ALL THE ANIMALS AND TEACH THEM TO DANCE!
NO, HARL... THAT'S NOT REVOLUTIONARY AT ALL. WE HAVE TO BE CONCISE IN OUR ACTIONS. DO IT FOR A CAUSE. MAKE A DIFFERENCE IN THE WORLD!
I SAY WE BREAK INTO THE DOWNTOWN GOTHAM ATRIUM, TAKE OUT ALL THE GUARDS, FORCE OUR WAY PAST THE CARETAKERS AND MAINTENANCE PERSONNEL... AND THEN...
...WE WATER ALL THE PLANTS!
PRETTY REVOLUTIONARY THERE, "CHE."
WHAT?! IT'LL BE FUN, TOO!
I KNOW, I KNOW!! WE CAN GO ROB THAT GOODY-GOODY BRUCE WAYNE AGAIN! I KNOW WHERE HE KEEPS ALL HIS FAVORITE RIDES.
OR... WE CAN GO SHOPPING.
FOR SHOES--AND FANCY HATS. MAYBE EVEN... ICE CREAM?

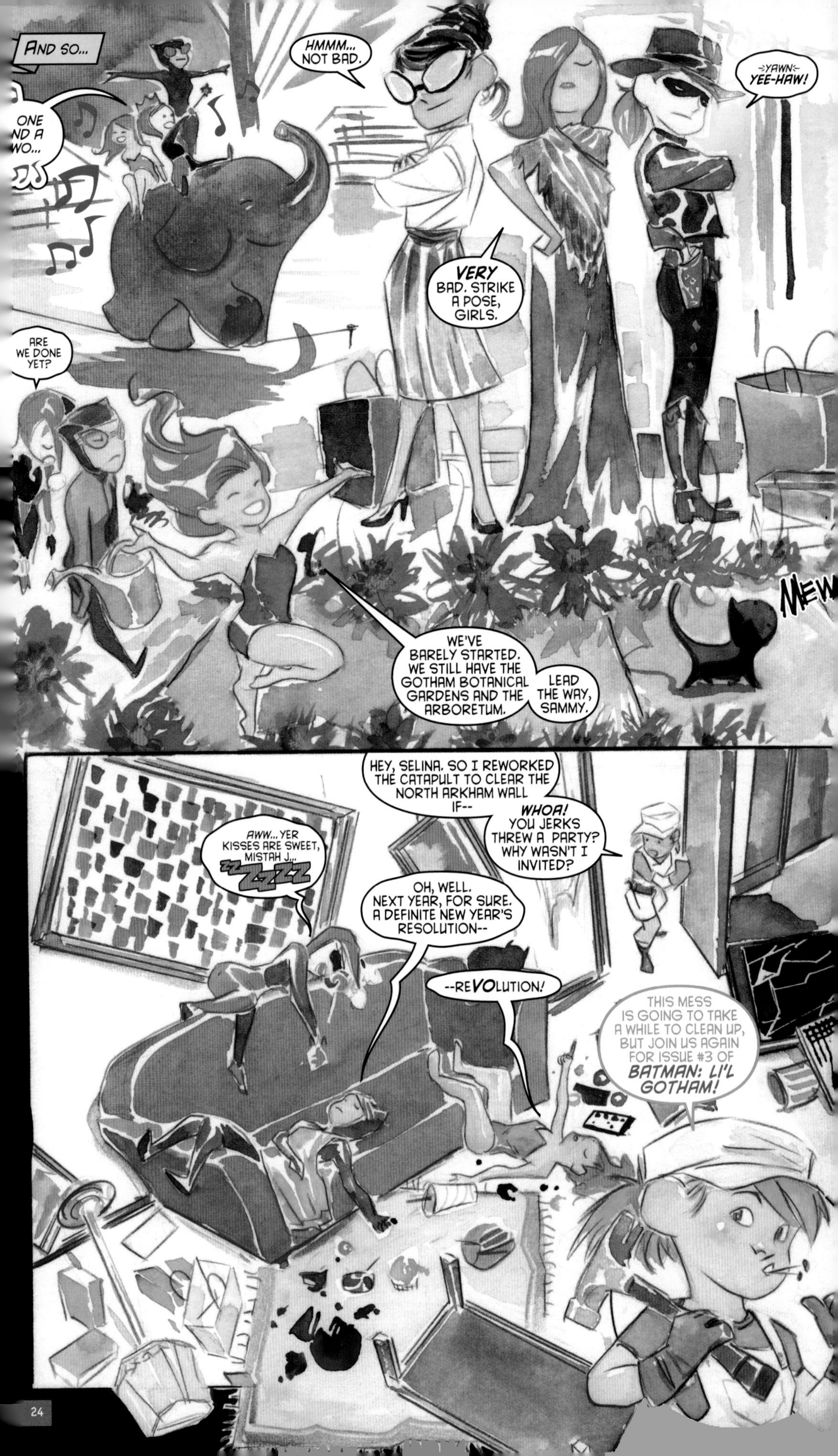

AND SO...
ONE
ND A
WO...
HMMM... NOT BAD.
>YAWN< YEE-HAW!
VERY BAD. STRIKE A POSE, GIRLS.
ARE WE DONE YET?
WE'VE BARELY STARTED. WE STILL HAVE THE GOTHAM BOTANICAL GARDENS AND THE ARBORETUM.
LEAD THE WAY, SAMMY.
MEW
HEY, SELINA. SO I REWORKED THE CATAPULT TO CLEAR THE NORTH ARKHAM WALL IF--
WHOA! YOU JERKS THREW A PARTY? WHY WASN'T I INVITED?
AWW... YER KISSES ARE SWEET, MISTAH J... ZZZZZ
OH, WELL. NEXT YEAR, FOR SURE. A DEFINITE NEW YEAR'S RESOLUTION--
--REVOLUTION!
THIS MESS IS GOING TO TAKE A WHILE TO CLEAN UP, BUT JOIN US AGAIN FOR ISSUE #3 OF BATMAN: LI'L GOTHAM!

CREATORS

DUSTIN NGUYEN — CO-WRITER & ILLUSTRATOR

Dustin Nguyen is an American comic artist whose body of work includes Wildcats v3.0, The Authority Revolution, Batman, Superman/Batman, Detective Comics, Batgirl, and his creator owned project Manifest Eternity. Currently, he produces all the art for Batman: Li'l Gotham, which is also written by himself and Derek Fridolfs. Outside of comics, Dustin moonlights as a conceptual artist for toys, games, and animation. In his spare time, he enjoys sleeping, driving, and sketching things he loves.

DEREK FRIDOLFS — CO-WRITER

Derek Fridolfs is a comic book writer, inker, and artist. He resides in Gotham--present and future.

GLOSSARY

apparently (uh-PAIR-ent-lee)--appearing to be real or true

atrium (A-tree-uhm)--the main or central room of a house that is open to the sky at the center and usually has a pool for the collection of rainwater

etiquette (ET-i-ket)--the rules of the proper way to behave

heckle (HEK-uhl)--to interrupt with questions or comments usually with the intention of annoying or hindering

medley (MED-lee)--a musical composition made up of a series of songs or short musical pieces

momentous (moh-MENT-uhss)--very important or significant

revolution (rev-oh-LOO-shuhn)--an overthrow or the replacement of an established government or political system

seclusion (sek-KLOO-zhuhn)--solitude, or a state of being alone

sponsoring (SPON-ser-ing)--supporting a cause or goal, financially or otherwise

struggle (STRUH-guhl)--to proceed with difficulty or with great effort

VISUAL QUESTIONS & PROMPTS

1. Each villain travels over Gotham City in a different way. What does each villain's method of travel say about them? How do they fit their personalities?

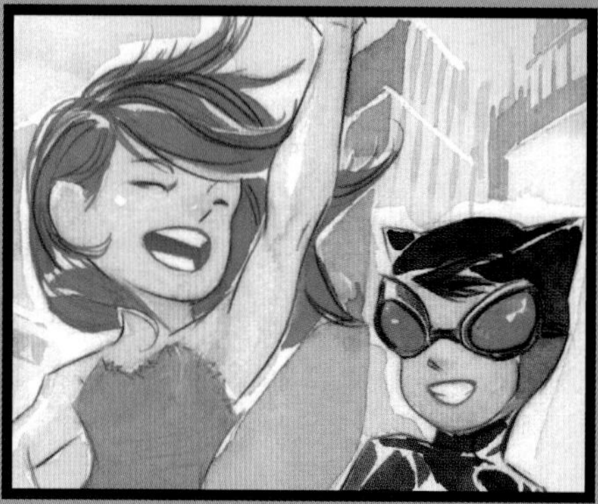

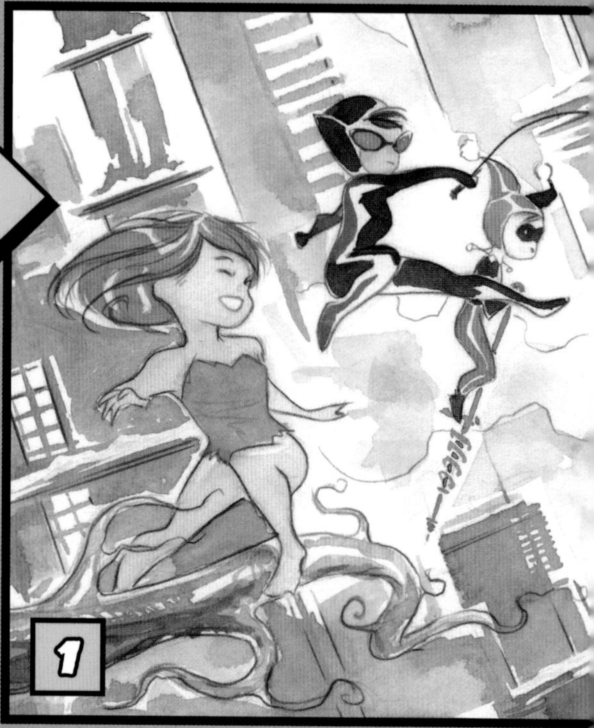

1

2. Based on her facial expression, how do you think Selina [Catwoman] feels about what Poison Ivy has to say?

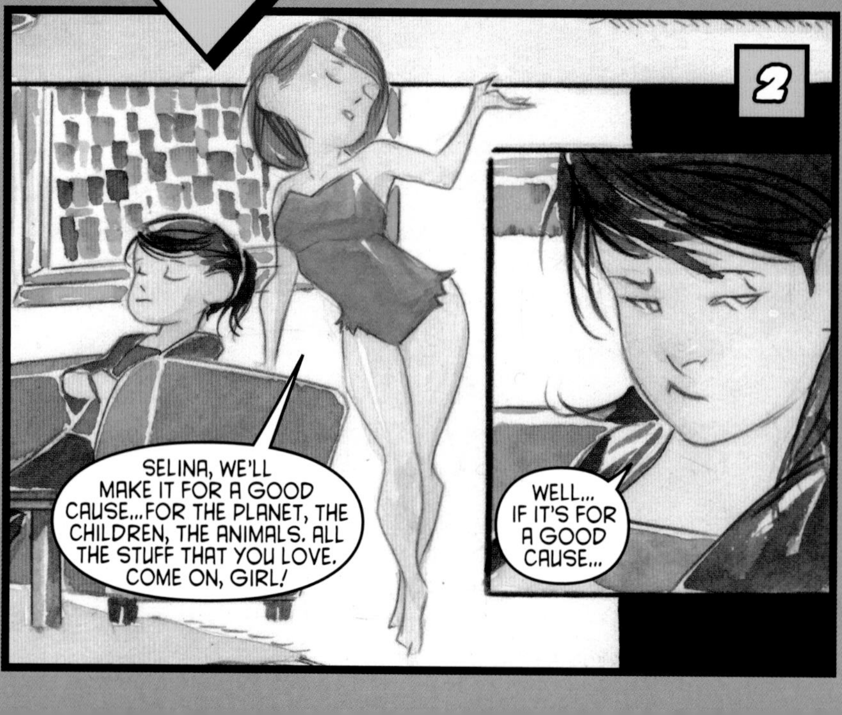

2
SELINA, WE'LL MAKE IT FOR A GOOD CAUSE...FOR THE PLANET, THE CHILDREN, THE ANIMALS. ALL THE STUFF THAT YOU LOVE. COME ON, GIRL!
WELL... IF IT'S FOR A GOOD CAUSE...

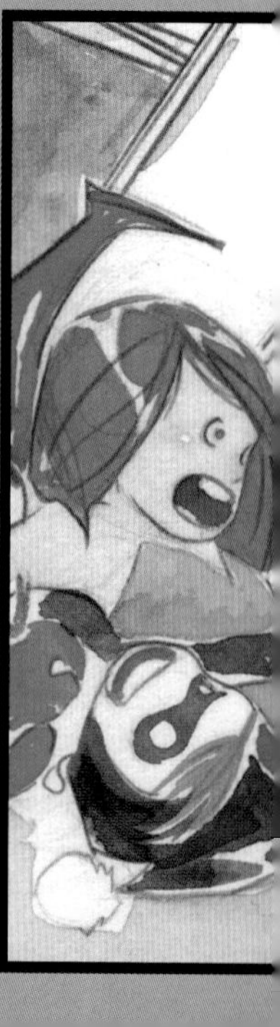

3. Did the events in this panel actually happen? Why or why not? Do you think Mr. Freeze would be happy doing any of these jobs?

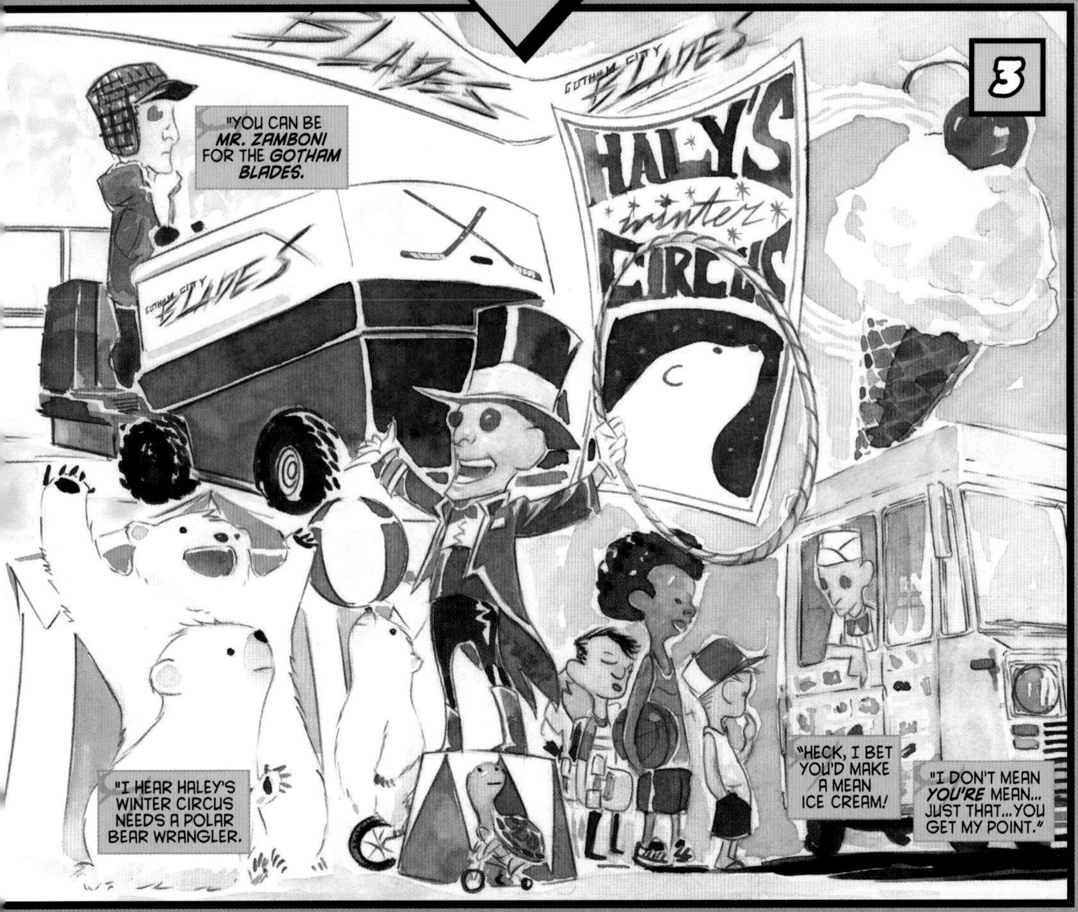
3
"YOU CAN BE MR. ZAMBONI FOR THE GOTHAM BLADES.
"I HEAR HALEY'S WINTER CIRCUS NEEDS A POLAR BEAR WRANGLER.
"HECK, I BET YOU'D MAKE A MEAN ICE CREAM!
"I DON'T MEAN YOU'RE MEAN... JUST THAT... YOU GET MY POINT."
HALY'S winter CIRCUS
GOTHAM CITY BLADES

4. Why does the panel look like this? Who is watching Catwoman?

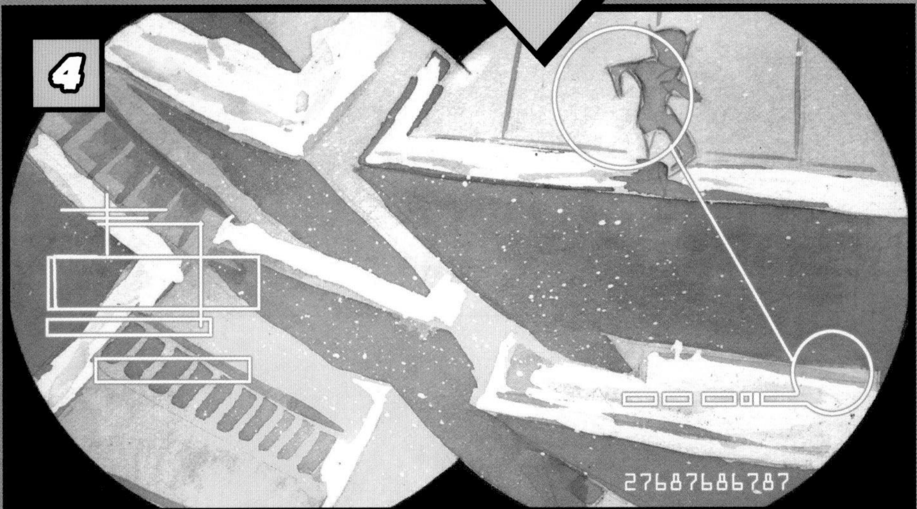
4
27687686787

BATMAN™
LI'L GOTHAM

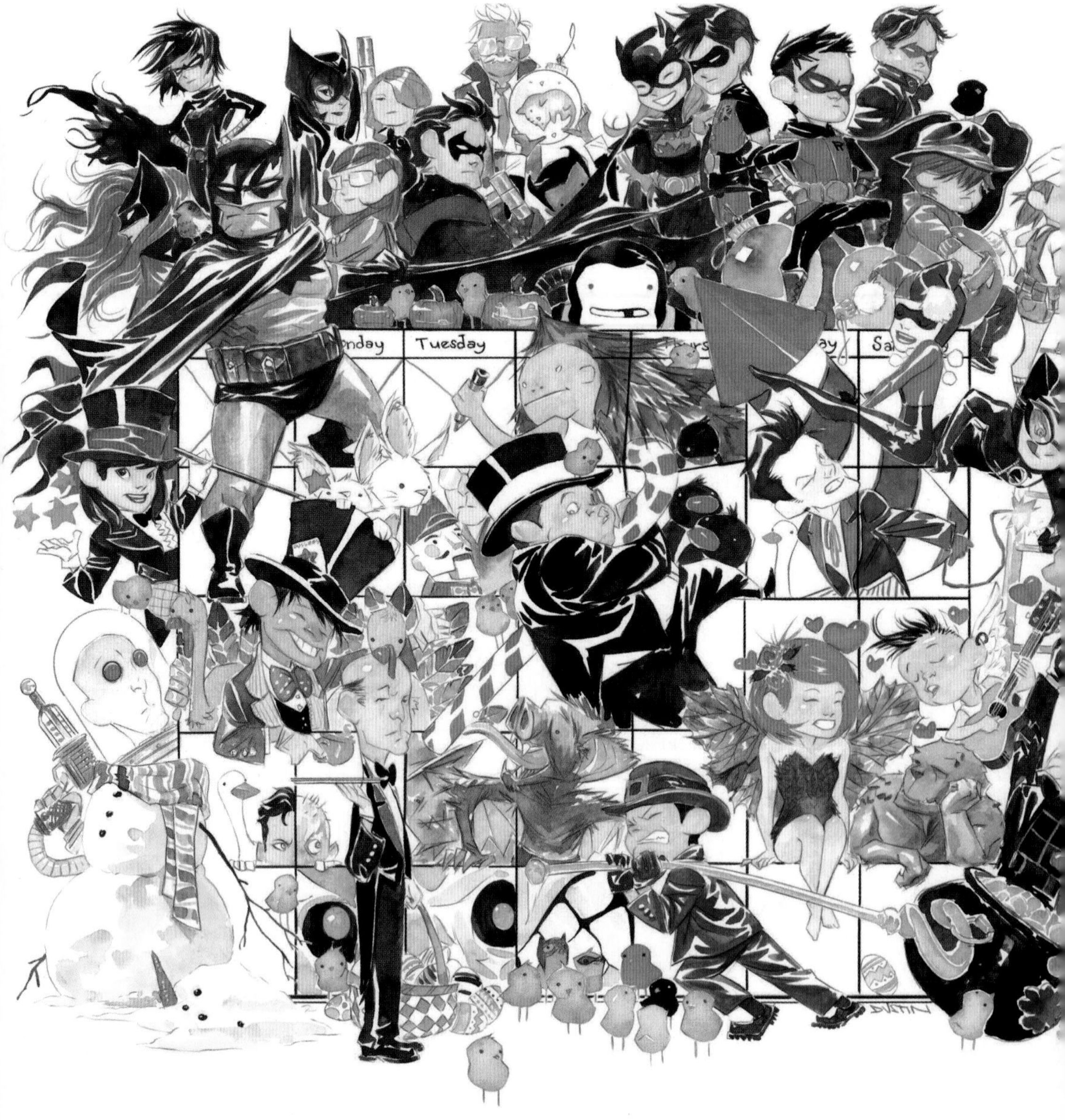
Tuesday

READ THEM ALL!

BATMAN
LI'L GOTHAM
HALLOWEEN AND THANKSGIVING

DC COMICS
BATMAN
LI'L GOTHAM
CHRISTMAS AND NEW YEAR'S EVE
NGUYEN • FRIDOLFS

DC COMICS
BATMAN
LI'L GOTHAM
NGUYEN
FRIDOLFS
VALENTINE'S DAY AND THE LUNAR NEW YEAR

BATMAN
LI'L GOTHAM
T. PATRICK'S DAY AND EASTER
NGUYEN • FRIDOLFS

DC COMICS
BATMAN
LI'L GOTHAM
NGUYEN
FRIDOLFS
APRIL SHOWERS AND CINCO DE MAYO

DC COMICS
BATMAN
LI'L GOTHAM
NGUYEN
FRIDOLFS
MOTHER'S DAY AND FATHER'S DAY

only from...

STONE ARCH BOOKS™
a capstone imprint www.capstonepub.com

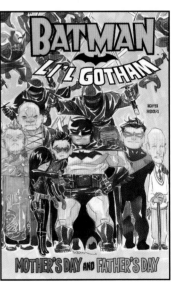

BATMAN™
LI'L GOTHAM

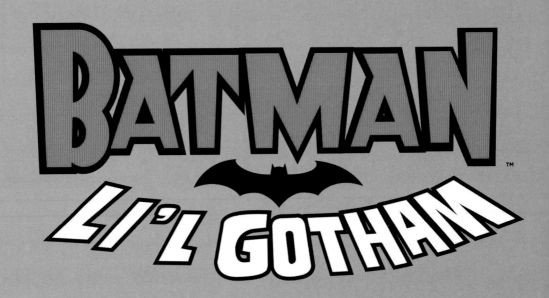